Northern Lightning

The Green Star Lake Series

Robert Checkwitch

Contents

CHAPTER 1

The Sentencing Circle

Jimmy was being held at the band detention room the Chief and council in Green Star Lake knew he had been running drugs into the community for most of the winter, and they were deciding what was to be done. It seemed to Jimmy that the RCMP and the band constables were taking their time to decide his fate. Everyone knew he couldn't cause more trouble while he sat in detention.

Theresa, his former girlfriend, visited him several times and often brought their son Chance. Jimmy was glad to see her, but there were times when he felt uncomfortable about her being pregnant by another young man in Winnipeg. Jimmy was no longer angry with Theresa because he knew he had been the one who had messed up the relationship with his criminal activities, drinking, drugs and violence. He accepted that the relationship had changed, that Theresa had decided to finish her school in Winnipeg, but she was there for him now, sitting patiently discussing the possibilities, appealing to chief and council or doing nothing and try to wait everyone out.

The trouble between Jimmy and the chief went back more than a few years but got serious three years ago when he tried to burn down the band office. It was 6 months in juvenile detention that time. It had been the end of a long streak of trouble that started when he was 10 years old.

"I figure they're going to pass a band council resolution to get me out of the community, that or jail," he told Theresa.

"I don't know Jimmy. A BCR forcing you out of the community is pretty serious. I can only remember that happening once or twice."

"It's the fastest way to get rid of me."

"They won't have to, if they decide to charge you, right?"

"Yeah, but I know they don't like to see us charged and put away in jail out of the community. They'd rather deal with it here."

"It's true. People don't want to depend on a court from outside. Maybe the chief would like that, but you've still got a few people on your side."

Jimmy laughed. "Oh yeah, my grandmother and my uncle Peter."

"No, some band councilors."

"Theresa. Come on. Not this time."

"Well, something has to happen," she told him.

"The RCMP will have to charge me or let me go. They can't hold me like this much longer."

Theresa knew that there was not a chance that Jimmy was going to walk away from this.

"At least you got your grade 10 before they picked you up."

"That was funny. Go to graduation, get my diploma, at seventeen, walk outside the school and get and get taken into detention. I bet that was the first time that's ever happened."

"We were all pretty shocked," she told him.

"For sure. I hadn't done anything for two or three months before that. Someone must have turned me in."

Chance toddled over to Jimmy and crawled up on his lap. Jimmy held him against his chest. "I never want to see you in here, Chance."

"I hope not, Jimmy. Don't even say that."

Jimmy smiled at her. "So, when's the baby coming?"

"Supposed to be in about 19 days."

Jimmy wanted to know if the father had been in contact with Theresa. "You heard from Keith?"

"Yep. He phones every week. Lots of questions. He has lots to say, but he's not having to do all the work."

Jimmy thought about that. "Well, he did some of the work, eh. You're pregnant, Theresa."

She gave him a playful smack on the side of the head.

"You going back to Winnipeg for grade 12, for sure?" he asked.

"I hope so. I'll be a few weeks late. Mom's going to have a big job this year, taking care of the baby"

"You sure you want to leave a new baby?"

"If I don't go back this year, I might never go back. That's what I'm most afraid of."

Jimmy understood.

Jimmy's grandmother came every day with food, often just sitting with him, saying very little. Often Peter came with her.

Vincent, came as well, although Jimmy was not very pleased to see him. Vincent had arrived in Green Star Lake last year with his mother, after being absent from the community for many years. Vincent was gay, and even though Jimmy tried to ignore this, he had not been able to overcome the fact of Vincent's lifestyle. Vincent never gave up trying to become a good friend to Jimmy, but there were days when Jimmy said little or nothing to him. A few times Jimmy told Vincent he was tired and asked him to leave. That didn't stop Vincent from visting.

Jimmy didn't know that Paul, the community shaman and medicine man, had met with chief and council twice to explore ways to deal with his situation beside. Chief and council knew that Paul had a relationship with Jimmy and had been discussing with Jimmy traditional ways to deal with his troubled life. Chief and council listened respectfully to his ideas. Paul suggested a sentencing circle be arranged with

members of Chief and council, three elders, a band constable, Jimmy and an RCMP officer.

Paul explained to Jimmy how the sentencing circle would work. "You will have a chance to speak as long as you want in the sentencing circle." He told Jimmy who would attend and how a decision would be reached. "People will be allowed to speak, but the circle will recommend a sentence that everybody will need to agree on, Jimmy. You can't be forced to be part of the circle if you don't want to be there, but then you will go through the regular court way. What do you think?"

Jimmy thought about it and knew that he would much prefer doing that to landing up in jail or having the band pass a band council resolution that would force him out of the community.

"Sure. Definitely." Anything to get out of here, Jimmy thought to himself

It took until the end of July before a decision was made. Jimmy was to spend two months in the bush with his fishing gear and a few basic supplies and was not to return before the middle of November. There was to be no contact with anyone, except one visit from Paul midway through the sentence. When Paul visited Jimmy they discussed the sentence. "I think it's a good decision," Paul told him. "The vision quest that we talked about could be part of this."

Jimmy's grandmother thought two months was too long to be in the bush without a boat and no contact with the community. She worried about the danger to Jimmy if he were injured. The Chief thought the sentence was too short and pushed for a term until Christmas. The band councillors, in the end, were satisfied with the length and the fact that the decision had been made by the community.

A few days before Jimmy was to leave, Theresa visited with Chance. As she sat watching him she felt a mixture of thoughts run through her head. Was she still in love with him? Will her new baby be okay? Will Keith be waiting for her in Winnipeg? Can she handle school? Will she be able to leave her two children? Will Jimmy survive the bush or take off? Will she have the strength to make it through the year? Will Keith support her or make it difficult for her to keep her baby in Green Star Lake? Theresa and Jimmy didn't say much to each other that last night. Theresa could tell Jimmy was going to the space he always retreated to when he faced hard times—that tough core that shut out the world around him where he could rely on himself, expecting nothing from anybody else, and focusing on the challenge in front of him. Theresa had seen it many times since he was a little boy. That fierceness. The place where nobody could touch him.

When Vincent visited that last night, he was on the verge of tears.

The next morning, Paul arrived, carrying a small leather pouch of traditional medicines and herbs.

"Use these when you need, like we talked about in the past," he told Jimmy. They arranged the time and place for Paul's one visit with Jimmy in the bush. Paul told Jimmy that his time in the bush would be an extended self-examination and voyage of discovery. A unique vision quest.

"You're going to be fine, Jimmy," Paul told him. "You're ready for this."

"I know. Time to get away from here for a while."

Jimmy was released on a hot day at the beginning of August. He refused all the food he was offered except a small package from his grandmother. His grandmother, Vincent and a band constable were there, but Theresa and Chance were not. Jimmy wondered about that. He had expected she would be there with Chance.

Vincent tried to give him his miniature music player.

Jimmy told him, "I can't take that, Vincent."

"Why not? It'll keep you in the zone."

Jimmy ignored him. Vincent was using his strange expressions again.

When Jimmy saw that his grandmother was upset, he put his arms around her and pulled her to his chest.

"Can you have a blueberry pie ready for me when I come back?"

Before Jimmy disappeared into the bush, he saw Zach standing off to one side, removed from everybody else. Zach had visited Jimmy twice in jail. Zach was 17 years old and was interested in talking to Jimmy only about his winter of drug running.Zach wanted to know the details.

Jimmy headed north, before angling west toward a point in the lake where he could set up camp. He stopped after two hours and took off his sneakers. His plan was to alternate between his gym shoes and his bare feet until they were tough enough to travel without anything on his feet. As the sun began to set, he found a spot where the shore gently sloped toward the lake. Deciding it would be his first base camp, he took out his hunting knife and started to build a shelter.

CHAPTER 2

Margaret's Decision

When Theresa woke up in the morning, she felt dizzy and quite ill. At noon, when she felt strong enough to make the short walk, she went to the clinic.

Theresa knew that Margaret, the head nurse at the clinic, had been concerned about her this past month. Margaret told Theresa to get ready for a trip to Winnipeg if her blood pressure and other vital signs showed that her health was in danger.

"The plane is here in two hours, Theresa," Margaret told her. "I've already made arrangements for you to be picked up and taken directly to the hospital. The van will take you home to pack."

"Am I going to be okay?" Theresa asked.

"Yes. The van will take you to the airport in an hour Go home and lie down until you're ready to leave. By supper you'll be in a hospital bed in Winnipeg. Don't worry, Theresa. The baby is going to be fine. We'll see you back here in 10 or 12 days with the new baby."

Theresa became worried immediately but put her trust in Margaret, who had been through plenty of emergencies.

After the clinic van took Theresa home, her mother immediately began to pack what Theresa would need for the trip. Her mother blocked out any possibilities other than the thought that she would be seeing her daughter back in Green Star Lake soon with a new baby.

Beatrice, Theresa's Cree counsellor in Winnipeg, was waiting for her when Theresa got off the plane. Beatrice took Theresa to the hospital late in the afternoon on Thursday, and at 3:12 am Saturday morning, Theresa had Natasha. At eight pounds and six ounces, she was healthy, with bright red cheeks, a full head of soft, black hair and Keith's eyes. Theresa tried to tell herself that she was only imagining the resemblance to Keith's eyes, that the baby was too young to show the similarity, but every time she looked into Natasha's eyes, she saw Keith

There was no denying it.

Keith visited the second day and hung around the hospital for several hours. Theresa saw his excitement and the love he was feeling for Natasha. As he sat next to the bed holding Theresa's hand, they talked about their daughter, about Theresa going back to school and about what they could all do together after Theresa and the baby left the hospital. After three days, Theresa had to tell Keith she was returning to Green Star Lake.

"I've got to Keith. I've only seen Chance for three or four weeks this summer. I want to spend the rest of the summer with him. You know that."

"I know I want to spend time with my daughter, Theresa. That's just as important to me."

"I know that, Keith, but I can't stay."

"Sure you could. You could stay with me and if you want to go home, my mom could take care of the baby until you get back."

"You sure don't know anything about babies. A mother is not going to be separated from her new baby so soon. What would that do to Natasha? You're not being realistic at all."

"I'm not being realistic. I'm not being realistic. Come on,

Theresa." Theresa could see he was beginning to get agitated. "You didn't even tell me you were pregnant. Now you're trying to separate me from my daughter."

"No, I'm not. I'm the mother, not you. Don't be ridiculous. Besides, you didn't even want to see me for a long time. You know that."

"That has nothing to do with our daughter."

"Yeah, you're all keen and loving now. What about in three months when you've got other things going on in your life? Now you're being ridiculous."

"Remember how you used to be with me when we first met? Just the way you're being with Natasha now."

Theresa thought he was going to yell at her. She saw his frustration as he gripped the railing of the bed with his tightly clenched hand, trying to control himself.

"It's true, Keith. You know that." Theresa reached out to hold his hand, but he pulled it away.

"So how am I going to get to see my daughter if she's up north and I'm here?"

"We'll have to see. We can't figure that out right now, can we? You're going to have to wait."

"Wait, wait." His voice began to rise. He shook his head. "I'm not going to accept this."

"Accept what, Keith? What do you have to accept?"

"Not seeing my baby. What do you think? What else?"

Theresa was afraid they were going to have a loud fight in the hospital. "Keith, I'm tired right now. I need to get some sleep. We can talk later."

"Talk about it later. You'll be saying that until you leave. I can see that."

Theresa was through talking. She closed her eyes and let her mind go to her children so she could shut Keith out. She heard him stomp out, muttering, "This isn't going to work."

Bruce, Vincent and Arielle talked to Theresa on their cell phones. They were excited and happy for her. After their conversation with Theresa, the three friends walked down the road together. It was a warm, sunny day in August, a time when the black flies and mosquitoes began to disappear. and the heat gave way to cool breezes and the aroma of late summer. It was Arielle's favorite time of the year.

"So are you going to split, Bruce?" Vincent asked.

"Yeah, pretty sure."

"Take the big bird out and go to university?"

"Yep, looks like."

"You going with him, or are you going to put it on cruise control up here, Arielle?" Vincent asked.

Arielle didn't answer, but Bruce did. "I hope so. I'm trying to convince her to leave with me."

Vincent laughed. "Yeah. Convince Arielle to do something.

Sure. I don't think you've got the combination to figure that out." All three laughed.

"That's not always true, Vincent," Arielle protested. "I don't always disagree with Bruce."

"Just most of the time, Arielle," Bruce told her.

"So you're not going to university, Arielle?" Vincent continued.

"Maybe I'll go back to work at the school," she answered.

"She'll probably be here 10 years from talking about going to university," Bruce said, laughing.

Vincent and Bruce saw that Arielle was beginning to get irritated. She changed the subject.

"What about you, Vincent?"

"No idea. At first I thought I'd go back to Toronto, then I'd go to Winnipeg for grade eleven, then maybe I'd stay here and take correspondence for grade 11, then maybe I'd wait to see what happened to Jimmy, then...then. You getting the feelin

I don't know my way to first base?"

"Why do you have to make a decision right now?" Bruce asked.

"I don't want to just hang around. That would be zip city. So did you get some scholarships, Bruce?"

"Naw, my marks weren't good enough. My scholarship was living with Lucas in the bush and my life in Green Star Lake. That's been worth more than a scholarship to university. I'll have to live at home. Not looking forward to that, though. I thought maybe me and Arielle could get a small place and go to school. I could get a part-time job."

Vincent and Bruce waited for Arielle to say something, but she remained quiet because she was thinking she'd rather be by herself at that moment.

"My dad's coming up for the last week before I leave. He's going to stay with Lucas and me at the cabin."

"Wow. I didn't expect that, Bruce." Vincent exclaimed.

"It's the last time he'll have a chance to see what my last eight months have been about."

"What does Lucas think about that?"

"You know Lucas. He'll get into the experience and go with the flow. He's kind of looking forward to another white man, I think. He doesn't talk about it. I'm sure my dad is going to do a lot of fishing. Should be interesting."

As Vincent broke off and headed towards his house, he waved to Arielle and Bruce and told them, "Sounds like the two of you got stuff to talk about. Don't be getting all ass-over teakettle with each other, eh?"

They both waved but said nothing to each other. They had done a lot of talking but always avoided the topic that was on their minds but never mentioned—the baby they had lost when Arielle was in a snowmobile accident. Once Bruce tried to bring it up, but Arielle talked about something else, as if she had not heard him. It was a huge barrier between them. unspoken, suppressed and hidden. Bruce needed to talk about the loss. Thinking about it immediately depressed him, kept him awake at night and led him to daydream almost every day.

But that part of his life was coming to an end. His main goal was to convince Arielle, the girl he loved, to go to university with him, no matter how vague she continued to be.

"When are you going to make up your mind, Arielle?

You've got to register for your courses by the end of next week."

"I don't know. I told you that. Why do you keep asking me?"

"Doesn't sound like you're going, but you just don't want to tell me. That's what I think."

"If I don't want to talk about it or tell anybody anything, or I haven't made up my mind, that's my business. It's not the first time you've put the pressure on me to do what you wanted." She stared at him.

He knew what she was talking about. He had put a lot of pressure on her to have the baby five months ago when she had been undecided. Her reminder immediately silenced him.

Bruce's father arrived the next week, and Arielle was relieved. After spending a lot of time with Bruce during the summer, she was glad to have more space for herself. Although she never considered breaking up with Bruce, the loss of the baby meant it might never be possible to feel that same connection w him. Besides, he was leaving in a week with his father, so the relationship would probably end then. If Bruce was never going to return to Green Star Lake, Arielle didn't see any point in making a decision that would upset both of them. Let time settle this. But she knew she would miss going out on the lake with him in her father's boat. Sitting in the middle of the lake, swimming together, just having fun. talking. joking with each other. She saw those pictures in her mind and was torn between the good memories and the bad.

Bruce's father and Lucas hit it off right from the beginning. Both were men of few words. They fished every day and in the evening sat in front of a fire, trying to communicate with limited words and many hand gestures. It was amusing for Bruce to watch.

On the last day, Bruce got up early and headed down the lake to have breakfast with Arielle before returning to get his dad for the trip to the airport. Bruce began to get emotional as soon as he got in the boat at Lucas' cabin. That last trip across the glassy lake would be burned into Bruce's mind for the rest of his life: the stillness, the reflection of clouds on the water, the smell in the air, the sight of Lucas running the outboard at the back of the boat, the sight of the cabin where he had spent the last eight months, the expanse of Green Star Lake. He tried to avoid looking at Lucas, but for a fraction of second their eyes met and Lucas gave him a quick smile of understanding. Bruce felt tears come to his eyes.

At the airport, the education councilor met Bruce and presented him with a pair of intricately beaded gloves, a gift from the community in recognition of his volunteer work at the school.

Arielle and Bruce held each other for a moment. "When am I going to see you again, Arielle?"

"We'll see each other again. You know that, Bruce."

Then Bruce and his father headed across the landing area to the plane.

When Bruce reached the top step of the stairs, he turned and took a long look at the community of Green Star Lake. As soon as he sat down in his seat, the tears began to flow and would not stop. His dad squeezed his shoulder.

"You were a very lucky guy to be able to share your life with everybody up here, Bruce. Lucas is a special man"

The plane taxied down to the end of the airstrip and made the turn into the wind before the pilot wound up the engines. As the plane passed the small terminal and began to lift, Bruce looked out the window and saw Arielle in her bright yellow jacket, waving at them. Then he closed his eyes. He began to accept that his relationship with Arielle might be over. He had no choice.

Vincent spent August trying to write music, but nothing came that satisfied him. It was one of the periods in every artist's life when no amount of effort and time would prove to be creative. Something had been lost. Some connection. Some set of circumstances. He sat at home struggling to write new songs. He went to the bush and sat by himself. He took his father's boat and headed for the middle of the lake, struggling to capture again what had come so easily a few months ago. At one point he screamed in frustration across the empty lake. It was pointless, and he knew it. The creative ideas had stopped as if someone had turned off a tap of water.

He talked to Arielle about it.

"Gone, just gone, 18 and I'm finished. Empty. All the ideas gone. I've sucked them all out, and I feel like an empty shell. Hollow inside. Like a vacuum cleaner was put inside my head and pulled everything out."

Arielle laughed out loud. "That's bullshit, Vincent."

"Bullshit. You don't what that feels like inside. Nothing left. Like cobwebs in the attic."

"Quit feeling so sorry for yourself. Why do you think you're so different from other artists?"

But what was the point in trying to describe the sinking feeling of depression he was beginning to sense coming on, like a heavy fog slowly dropping over him. Every day Vincent felt a little more smothered by it. His mother and father became concerned. Vincent often fell asleep when the sun rose and stayed in bed until late afternoon. When he could get alcohol, he went to the bush and drank by himself. He wondered how he could have felt so good about himself and his life a few months ago, only to descend into his present mood.

For Vincent, everything had changed. Jimmy was gone to the bush. Bruce had left for Winnipeg. Theresa had gone back to school in Winnipeg, and Arielle was talking about going to the University even though she would be late for her courses. Maybe it was those last days with Jimmy before he left for the bush. Near the end, Fred, the band constable, had told him that Jimmy preferred to be left alone in his detention, that he didn't want to talk to Vincent. He had been hoping that he and Jimmy might go to school in Winnipeg but now realized it had been an unrealistic fantasy that made his depression worse.

Arielle told him, "Give it a break, Vincent. Quit pushing the music for a while. Walk away from it for a while. Stop bugging yourself with it. Isn't that what people do when they're stuck?"

But Vincent couldn't give it a break. His music was all he had left. "Some days I get so pissed off with myself I just want to end it all."

Arielle went over to him and put her arms around Vincent. "Don't say anything more, Vincent. Don't, don't Vincent. You'll come out of it. Don't start talking like that. I couldn't take another loss like that."

"Okay, okay." Vincent immediately remembered that Arielle had lost her baby. "Maybe I just need a good boot in the ass instead of crying on your shoulder."

"Look at all the music you've written already, and you're still so young. Have you thought about going back to Toronto where all your friends are?"

Vincent shook his head slowly. "I don't know, Arielle."

"Afraid, Vincent?"

"Maybe. Why? I'm not sure. Look at you. You're willing to

go to Winnipeg by yourself."

"I know some people there. I'd have school. It's different. Maybe you've got to get your gay head out of here for while."

Vincent knew Arielle was not putting him down but trying to cheer him up. On the way home Vincent thought about their conversation. It picked him up for the moment, but the next afternoon when he woke up with a hangover, he was unable to get out of bed. He lay staring at the ceiling, urging his body to stand up.

CHAPTER 3

Zach

Jimmy had seen Zach at the school the year before but had only talked to him a few times. Zach mostly kept to himself when he was in the community, skulking around with his shoulders slumped forward and his gaze focused on the ground so as to avoid meeting the eyes of others. In school, he rarely responded when spoken to unless it was absolutely necessary. His preferred colour was black—black gym shoes, black T-shirt, black jeans, black baseball cap. Never a sliver of color. Zach was very thin and short, with wiry arms and wide eyes that were set deep into his angular, bony face. His eyes stared out with a strange mixture of sadness and ferocity. Often Jimmy saw Zach sitting by himself on the dock, staring across the lake for hours, as if he was waiting for someone or something to appear. A few times when Jimmy was getting ready to take out the boat, he tried to start a conversation with Zach, but only managed to get an "okay" or "not much," two answers that seemed to be all that was required to cover every situation for Zach.

After asking Zach if wanted to go fishing with him a couple of times and getting a "Naw," Jimmy decided to completely ignore him. The last time Jimmy pulled the boat into the dock,

Zach was lying on his back, staring at the sky, with his legs hanging over the edge of boards and dangling in the water.

When Jimmy unloaded the boat and left, Zach didn't move.

Jimmy knew that Zach had been sent home from school several times for refusing to do any work. He always seemed to be giving his teachers lots of attitude and silent rejections.

So Jimmy was stunned when, a week before he left for the bush, Fred asked him if he wanted to talk to Zach, who was waiting outside the jail.

"He wants to talk to you, Jimmy." Jimmy hesitated.

"I can tell him to come back."

"Let him in." Jimmy was curious about what Zach might want.

Zach sat across from Jimmy in the waiting room of the jail and said nothing.

Jimmy finally said, "So Zach, what?" "What?" Zach asked.

"What, what? You came here to stare at me? Maybe you should go."

They sat across from each other as if they were having a duel to see who would start the conversation first. Jimmy quickly tired of it and got up. "Well, thanks for dropping in, Zach. It's been really interesting." Then he got up to leave.

"No," Zach blurted out.

"No?" Jimmy turned to exit the room.

"Wait," Zach said loudly.

Jimmy stood at the door, staring at Zach silently.

"Don't go yet."

"What do you want, Zach? Why are you here?"

"Can you just sit down?"

"Don't tell me what to do." Jimmy continued to glare at Zach.

"I want to talk to you."

"What about?"

"Stuff, things."

"Stuff, things." Jimmy laughed.

"You know, about what you were doing last winter."

"What do you mean? About last winter?"

Zach didn't want to use the word "drugs", fearing Jimmy would lose his temper.

"Well...why you're in here."

"What do you mean? What the hell do you want?"

"I want to talk to you about how you did that."

"Did what?"

"You know. Sell stuff."

"You mean, like sell stuff that got me in here?" Zach nodded.

"Oh, drugs, drugs, is that it, Zach? How I run drugs. You want to be a drug runner, Zach? Is that it?" Zach gave Jimmy the smallest nod.

"Why? Why, Zach?"

"I'm interested."

"Cause you want to be like me. Make money. Go to jail. Is that it?"

Zach didn't answer, but Jimmy knew exactly what Zach was thinking. Zach was almost eighteen but Jimmy remembered how he was thinking when he himself was 11 or 12 searching for an easy route to deal with his anger and loneliness.

"Do you want to land up in here?" Jimmy was getting mad. He got up to leave. "Leave me alone," Jimmy said. "You're being stupid, Zach. An idiot. Go back to school."

Zach began to speak, but Jimmy just turned and walked out of the room. "Stupid, very stupid."

As he left, he heard Zach's last words. "You didn't think it was stupid."

As Jimmy made his way through the bush, he thought about that last time Zach visited before Jimmy left. So Zach was trying to copy him. Bizarre. Jimmy could tell that Zach would never have what it took to get into that life. He'd get eaten alive in the drug trade. Besides, he had no money and not a clue. He was just a young guy talking about some goofy idea, a dreamer thinking about easy money. Still, Jimmy wondered what it had taken for Zach to get up the nerve to come to detention when he had always been such a loner. Jimmy couldn't get the picture out of his mind of Zach sitting at the table, his skinny body slumped forward, his legs stretched out before him and his thin arms crossed over his chest.

With that haunted stare and hollow cheeks, he looked like a desperate animal. Jimmy thought Zach must have been disappointed with the few minutes they had spent together. Good.

But Zach wasn't disappointed at all. He had made up his mind about what he wanted to do, and just taking that first step had been good enough for the time being. He knew he'd be back to talk to Jimmy again. For sure.

CHAPTER 4

Arielle Leaves

One morning in the second week of September, Arielle walked into the kitchen to join her father, who sat drinking coffee and working on one of his nets. "I'm going out, Dad."

"When?" he asked surprised.

"Tomorrow."

"Tomorrow? Why so fast?"

"I'm already late for school. It started a week ago, and I've got to register, find a place to stay, get organized, see if they'll let me in."

Her dad sat in silence, trying to absorb what she was telling him. Finally he said, " Okay. What do we have to do? What about money?"

"I've got some money saved, and I'm going to the band this morning to see what they will do."

"I can help."

"No. Not yet. I'll let you know if I get stuck. Let's save that until I really need it."

She went to him and put her hand on his shoulder. "Are you going to be okay?"

"Of course. I knew it would happen one day. You went out to finish high school. Now it's university. I'm happy for you.

Your mother would have been happy, too."

Arielle went to the school to tell her principal and then walked to the band office. It was swift and final—no turning back now. She called her friend in Winnipeg and arranged to stay with her until she found a place of her own. All the thinking and worrying about the right thing to do was behind her now. Arielle was feeling good.

The next day, her dad and friends were at the airport when the plane landed.

"You going to be okay by yourself, Dad?"

"Oh sure. The last thing you should be worrying about is me right now. You go out, get settled and think about school and your new life. I'll be here when you get back at Christmas."

She turned to put her arms around him and laid her head on his chest. She could feel his heart beating as he held her tightly. The thought that often came to her at times like this was that her father would meet someone who would share her life with this good man. Just before she walked to the plane, he told her, "I know you're going to do great things, Arielle. Don't lose your determination."

"I won't, Dad."

Half-way to the plane, she stopped and turned to look back at him. He was standing like the rock he was, with his arms crossed, his feet spread apart and his head thrust toward her. She had no way of knowing that this would be the last time she would ever see him. It was the way she'd always remember him. That last image would never be erased from her memory—her father standing at the airport on that clear, sunny, beautiful day when the silver bird flew her out of Green Star Lake and into her new life.

The day before Jimmy left dentention, Zach had returned. Jimmy didn't really want to see him, but Fred persuaded him to speak to Zach for a few minutes.

"Do it, Jimmy. He hardly ever speaks to anyone else."

"I've got other things on my mind, Fred, but I want him to leave after a couple of minutes."

Zach looked as if he hadn't slept for a few days. Looking at his scrawny body, Jimmy wondered if Zach ever ate.

"You leavin' tomorrow, hey?"

"Yep."

"It'll be November before you're back."

"It'll go fast, Zach."

"I wish I could go with you."

"That's so crazy. What's the matter with you? Don't you have things you want to do? Like a life?"

"I've got something for you." Zach took a cloth from his pocket and unwrapped a small carving.

"It's to take with you."

"Did you make it?"

Zach stared at the floor. "Yeah. It's for good luck."

Jimmy could no longer be irritated with Zach. "Thanks, Zach. I'll take it with me."

"I've got to go, Jimmy. I hope you come back okay."

"I will, Zach."

"Maybe then we can talk about doing some things together."

At that point, Jimmy understood that Zach would not give up on the ideas he had going around in his head. Jimmy chose to ignore him.

"I'll see you when I get back, Zach." Zach turned without a word and left.

Jimmy began to wonder what would happen to Zach in the next few years, but soon his mind switched to the thought of leaving in the morning.

CHAPTER 5

Natasha

Theresa arrived back in Green Star Lake five days after Jimmy was back on his own.. Her mother and all her friends were at the airport, anxious to see the new baby. Theresa had taken the time to breast-feed Natasha just before leaving, and the baby was still sleeping when they landed. It was only when everybody was crowding around her that the baby woke up and began to cry.

Everybody wanted to hold the baby. "Look at all her hair."

"Her eyes are so beautiful, Theresa."

"She's so small," Chance told his mother. His grandmother had tried to explain about his new sister, who would be coming home when he next saw his mother, but he was feeling a mixture of confusion and happiness as he held onto Theresa's leg and pressed his face against her thigh. It was good to feel her hand rubbing the top of his head again. Hearing her voice, a feeling of warmth spread through his body.

When they got home, Theresa saw that her mother had everything ready for her return home—a new crib, a fresh coat of paint in her bedroom, and new baby clothing laid out on Theresa's bed. Theresa was more than happy to be home. Margaret came over and was clearly relieved that Theresa was home safely with a healthy baby, after the worry of those last few days before Theresa's flight to Winnipeg. Sitting in the kitchen with her head resting on the back of the chair, Theresa slowly fell asleep with Natasha in her arms. Her last thought before she fell asleep was how she had left Winnipeg without telling Keith. It brought her both sadness and a sense of freedom.

The next day, Theresa talked to her mother about feeding Natasha. "You know I"m going out again in five or six weeks, so you'll have to start bottle-feeding her pretty soon. I'm going to be worried about her going on the bottle so soon." Theresa smiled sadly.

Her mother knew how badly her daughter wanted to grad-uate from high school and how tough it would be to leave Chance and Natasha.

"Maybe we could wait a week or two," her mother said. " I think that would be better."

"I don't want her to get too used to breast-feeding. I want her to know that the bottle is going to be part of her life, so I'd like to start pretty soon."

"Okay, I'll get up at night and do it so you can get some rest."

"Yeah, I'm pretty exhausted."

It was the first time she saw dark rings under her daughter's eyes. It saddened her to see Theresa growing up so soon, just 18 years old and carrying so many responsibilities. "I know how difficult it's going to be for you to fly out," her mother said, "but it's going to be okay. Your father and I can handle everything."

Theresa was glad to see that her father had slowly got his life back together after spending three years in Winnipeg, where he had fallen into a life of drinking. She remembered the day when she and Jimmy had picked him up in Brandon and had managed to get him on the plane to Green Star Lake, where her mother's love and strength eventually brought him back to his previous self. Now he had a good relationship with

Chance, and Theresa knew he would be a loving grandfather to Natasha when she was back at school. It was a relief to know that her mother wouldn't be caring for the children by herself.

Theresa had expected to see Jimmy when she returned, but he had already left. He'd been gone for a week. Although she wouldn't be seeing him until Christmas, she was happy that he wouldn't be going to jail. She wondered what Jimmy would be doing when he came out of the bush. She knew that too much time on his hands could mean more trouble.

He had no chance to get his grade 11 that year. Would he ever? Hardly a day passed that he was not on her mind. When she worried about whether he could take all that time in the bush by himself, she reminded herself that Jimmy liked nothing better than to prove to everybody that his toughness could beat anything thrown at him. She would like nothing better than to see him walk out of the trees in November. Many days she tried to see that picture in her mind.

Theresa had spent August resting and recovering, playing with Chance, reading to him and talking with Vincent, Arielle and Bruce. When Theresa could get away, the four of them would sit around discussing their lives, their worries, their dreams and where they would be in a couple of years.

Bruce, Theresa and Arielle were concerned about Vincent, who seemed to have lost his spark and sense of humour. They were not used to a Vincent who was so quiet. They talked about him when he wasn't present, searching for a way they could bring him back from his silence and his way of avoiding their interest. The four knew they would soon be parting ways, so they tried to hold onto the connection that had become so important to them. Their lives were all so different, and they were all going in separate directions. They knew it as they looked at each other that last day together, before Bruce flew out. Would those days ever return?

It took Theresa four weeks before she felt comfortable about putting Natasha completely on the bottle. In the back of her mind, she knew that when she gave up breast-feeding, it would be time to leave. By the middle of September, Theresa knew she had to get on the plane, or she would probably lose her chance to graduate from grade 12.

Her mom asked one morning, "When are you leaving?" Theresa didn't answer.

"Your father and I can do this. You don't have to worry."

"I know that, Mom. I'm not worried about that."

"What then?"

"I'm worried about being away from Chance and Natasha so much."

"Do you want to be sitting here four or five years from now, frustrated and angry with yourself that you didn't try it?"

"No."

"So?" Theresa knew that her mother was telling her to leave. Now. She wouldn't say it though.

Theresa got up from the table and took Natasha and Chance for a walk. When she returned, she told her mother, "Okay, Friday, Mom."

Her mother came over and put her arms around her daughter. "That's good."

Friday, on the plane heading for Winnipeg, Theresa knew she had made the right decision. She was ready to face the year and Keith.

As summer ended, Zach had little to do. Often he would wander around the community, stopping occasionally to talk to a few people but leaving quickly when those conversations made him uncomfortable. It wasn't that other young people ignored him or didn't want to talk to him. They simply found it hard to figure Zach out. He sensed that as soon as he joined a group, a tense edge emerged, so he left quietly. As September approached, he knew school would become an issue between him and his father, who wanted him to stay in school even if Zach was having a lot of difficulty. He dreaded the thought of those long days, struggling to read and facing failure at his age. It was embarrassing and discouraging. He felt as if he were watching a bad movie over and over, and he was the losing star.

He wished he could start traveling—just get on the plane and keep going from place to place until he decided what he wanted to do with his life. Yeah. He could just keep going, heading out to who knows where. Some days he lay on his bed with his eyes closed, picturing himself going down never-ending highways and through busy cities with towering buildings of glass, like those he'd seen on TV.

When he'd walk out of the house, he would realize the radical difference between what he saw in his head and what he saw in Green Star Lake. His reality—small houses, trees, the lake, miles and miles of water and bush pulled him in a direction very different from his daydreams of the city.

One thing Zach did know was that he'd never be able to travel those other roads without money.

It was the only way. It wasn't going to happen through school, and that's why his relationship with Jimmy was so important to his goal. He knew that Jimmy had not taken him seriously during those conversations at the jail because he saw Zach as a stupid, innocent kid.

Zach knew he'd have to do something to prove to himself and Jimmy that he was serious and had it in him to take the next step.

He'd have to start with some action that would prove to Jimmy that he was through talking and was tough enough to be an outlaw, a criminal ready to take on any risk beyond what Jimmy coul dpossibly imagine—beyond Jimmy's accomplishments at the same age.

One night he broke into the building at the airport, looking for cash. He found nothing but wasn't disappointed, because he had started and had not been caught. He was on his way. His next targets would be the two stores in Green Star Lake. When he thought about getting caught, he had no concern, since then they might think about sending him out. Just like school. Cause enough trouble and they'd suspend you for a few days. Yeah.

That made sense to Zach.

CHAPTER 6

In the Bush

J immy spent his first days in the bush getting accustomed to hunting and fishing for food.

After a few days, he decided to establish a daily routine, starting with a swim, a clean-up, and frying fish in a small pan he'd brought. His uncle had taught him several years ago how to build a snare with wire, so he could get rabbits as part of his diet. Still, he found it a challenge to get his first rabbit in the snare. His diet consisted mostly of fish, berries and rabbit when he could get them. Paul had explained that white and yellow berries were usually those that should be avoided, but if Jimmy was unsure he could put the berry to the end of his tongue to see how bitter it was. It was best to leave the bitter ones if he didn't want to get sick. It would be a few weeks before he would trap beaver as part of his food source, since summer had never been a time when the community ate beaver. Once the colder weather came at the end of October, there would be more fat on the beavers, and the eating would be better. He would wait until the temperatures dropped much lower and snow was in the air before he started eating his favorite meal.

He was surprised how much of the day was taken up with basic jobs just to survive. He had been taught by Paul about the various plants that could be used as well and this added variety to his diet. All things considered, it was a pretty healthy selection of food, which gave him strength and a feeling of satisfaction. That first stop was where he built his first base camp. He erected a shelter of poles and branches with a bed of boughs. Jimmy wanted to feel he had a secure location he could return to when things got rough or when he needed to rest up if he got sick or injured. He stayed at that spot for a week before he felt the urge to explore new territory, both out of interest and to find a source of food. Often he was on the move for several days, rising in the morning feeling pushed by some unknown force to cover more ground, and stopping only to eat and sleep under the stars.

When he reached a spot beside a lake or river he particularly liked, he would build another shelter, set up camp, trap, fish and rest. When it rained, he'd spend more time inside one of the well built shelters, often just lying on his back, and wearing only a pair of shorts, thinking, dreaming and letting his mind wander through the worlds he had come to welcome or thoughts about Chance, Theresa and his life. Soon his days were filled with a familiar routine and a sense of achievement. Gone was any anger, frustration or self-doubt. What remained was a reliance on himself and the world around him and a kind of solitary peace that shut out the memory of his previous life.

It took Jimmy a while to find the spot where he had agreed to meet Paul, where a stream entered the lake. Jimmy was waiting on a flat rock shelf the next evening, when he heard the 20 horsepower off in the distance. The sun was setting just above the trees, throwing a reflected, bright-orange glare on the surface of water behind Paul's slowly approaching boat. Jimmy stood up and waved to Paul.

Later, they sat beside a fire frying the pickerel Jimmy had caught that evening while Paul boiled the rice he had brought with him.

"How have you been, Jimmy?"

"I'm good, Paul, a little bored some days, but pretty good and busy."

"Busy?"

"Yeah, busy." Jimmy explained his schedule. "I figure it's the best way for me to get through the days. Keep moving. Keep busy."

"I understand. Push yourself for a while, then rest for a short time."

"It works. It's made me strong."

They talked well into the evening. Before they slept, Paul took out a small bag with finely ground plants. "Some nights, I'd like you to try these when you're rested and you're sitting beside a lake or river as the sun is going down. When your head is feeling good. Clear. They're good for your body and. spirit

"Okay. Anything else?"

"I brought you a small pad. I'd like you to write about the things you're thinking and doing. Can you do that?"

"I guess so. But why?"

"I just think it would be a good idea," the shaman told him. "It would be good to do on those days when it rains, and you're sitting in one of your shelters. It might be something you're glad you did years from today. Something that might be valuable for you."

"Okay, I'll try." But Jimmy knew he had never liked writing at school, at home or anywhere. He wondered why Paul was asking him to do this. Where was this taking him?

A couple of evenings after Paul left, Jimmy made his way across some large boulders to the middle of the main river running into Green Star Lake. As he listened to the water rushing past, only a few inches from his body, he began to take the mixture Paul had left with him. He soon moved into a trance more powerful and moving than any he had ever experienced. He saw brilliant images from early in his life, pictures that looked as if they were hundreds of years old. A continuous flash of rapidly changing images alternated between colours and black-and-white. Old and new images were all meshed together. Animals appeared, vying for his attention, trying to talk to him. At times they were silent, as if they were waiting for Jimmy to get up, move, make a decision. At other times, they circled Jimmy, calling out to him. Sometimes there was a brilliant array of stars in the background; sometimes a blinding sun.

As the sun began to rise in the morning, Jimmy awoke to find that he was still lying on the rock in the middle of the river. He felt incredibly hungry and full of energy.

In the mornings after such nights, he would sit beside the fire, cooking and thinking about as many of the visions as he could remember. Over the days he came to understand that something was expected of him—that he had to make a decision.

Jimmy made the circuit of his five shelters twice. When it rained, he sat in one of his shelters writing furiously in the notebook that Paul had left. He was still in the bush at the end of November, past the length of time he was expected to fulfill.

Back in Green Star Lake, Jimmy's grandmother started to worry as the snowy weather began. She talked to her brother, Peter, who wouldn't admit he was also beginning to get concerned.

One day Paul visited Jimmy's grandmother.

"I know that you're worried," he told her, "but don't be. Jimmy is strong, and I know he'll walk out of that bush. I know he will."

"But when?" she asked.

"Soon," Paul answered with confidence. "Soon."

Two days later, Jimmy strode out of the trees behind his grandmother's home. When he came through the door, she was sitting at the table, beading a pair of moccasins.

"So where's my blueberry pie?" he asked in Cree. "You promised me that."

She got up and gently put her arms around him without saying a word.

Jimmy slept most of the next three days, getting up only to eat and drink water. Many members of the community visited, but not the chief. Some things never change, thought Jimmy, but inside for the first time, he had less anger towards the leader of his community.

CHAPTER 7

Arielle Goes Home

When Arielle landed in Winnipeg, she was met by her friend from Green Star Lake, a child-care worker at a family centre in the downtown core of the city.

Early the next day, Arielle headed to the University to register for her education courses.

She explained to the woman in the registrar's office why she was late. "I couldn't get out before this. I've come a long way to do this."

"I'm sorry, but it's too late to start," the woman told her.

"You'll have to wait until the next term after Christmas."

"I'll work," Arielle promised. "I'll catch up."

The discussion went back and forth for 10 minutes, with Arielle refusing to accept "no" for an answer.

"I'm really sorry," she was told.

Finally, Arielle left the office and wandered around and through the buildings on the campus. Eventually, she entered a large library with windows overlooking trees and lawns on the grounds, where groups of students rushed back and forth. She felt good being there, as if she belonged. It depressed her to come all this way only to be disappointed. What now?

As she was about to leave, three Aboriginal students passed by. One of the girls stopped and came over to Arielle.

"Hey, what's up?"

"Not much," Arielle answered.

"You look down."

"I look down?" Arielle asked. "Yep, what's wrong?"

Arielle wasn't about to confide in someone she didn't know, but the girl persisted.

"We're going for lunch. Why don't you come with us?"

Why not? thought Arielle. After sitting down for lunch with her three new friends, who were from different communities in the north, Arielle finally told them about her problem.

"You've got to go see Emily at the registrar's office. She's from up north, just like us. If anybody can solve your problem, it's Emily. When we're finished here, I'll take you over to meet her."

At the registrar's office, Arielle explained her situation, and Emily told her to come back early the next day.

When she returned the next day, she saw some course outlines and schedules sitting on Emily's desk.

"They'll let you in," Emily told her, " but you've only got a limited number of courses to choose from. Some of them you're going to have to take. You'll have to accept it."

Arielle was thrilled. "That's great, Emily. Of course I'll take whatever I have to so I can get in. Does that mean I can start today or tomorrow?"

"This morning. Your first class is at 10:30. Psychology. I'll speak to all your professors and explain your situation, but I'd suggest that you go see them after the first class. Some will be okay with it. Some might not. It'll be up to you to prove to them you're willing to work and catch up."

"Definitely. I won't let you down, Emily."

"Not me, Arielle. Yourself. Keep in mind that your doing it

for yourself."

After a week of going to school during the day and working hard every night on her courses, Arielle began to catch up to the other students. She found herself in the groove of university life, and she loved it.

One day she saw a notice on a bulletin board: "Three students with a large house looking for a fourth to share expenses. Good friends, and a comfortable house. $300.00 per month, utilities included."

Arielle phoned the house and went to meet the three students the same evening. Two female students and a guy from Spain lived in the house. The next day, she moved into her new room. It had one single bed, one desk, a set of drawers and a small shelf. One of the girls gave her a set of sheets, a towel and a pillow until she could go shopping. Arielle was happy in her new room and slept well that night.

By the end of September, she had caught up to the students in her classes.

She had seen Bruce only a couple of times. He asked why she had been avoiding him. When Arielle told him it was because school was important and she needed to catch up. Bruce knew it wasn't the only reason, and it was pointless to pressure her. It had never worked in the past. Never.

At the end of October, she came home from school to find a message one of her room-mates had left on the kitchen table:

"Phone Margaret at the nursing station. She said it was important."

When Margaret came to the phone, she told Arielle she wanted Arielle to speak with her grandfather.

"Why? What's going on, Margaret?"

"The van has left to go get him, Arielle. We'll phone you back in five minutes."

Arielle knew her grandfather didn't have a phone.

"Why won't you tell me anything?" She began to get a bad feeling.

A few minutes later, her grandfather phoned. "I'm sorry. I have bad news, Arielle."

"No, no, don't tell me. Don't tell me it's dad."

"I'm sorry. He didn't come back last night or the night before. They found his boat yesterday and your father this morning. Such a good man to lose." Arielle couldn't speak.

"The band has bought you a ticket so you can come home as soon as you're ready. We'll be waiting for you at the airport."

Arielle got off the phone and went to her room. Her roommates knocked on the door until midnight, but she refused to open it.

"We're worried about you. Open the door or we're going to break in."

When Arielle finally opened the door and they learned what had happened, they put their arms around her and held her tight.

"You going back? When?"

"Tomorrow."

"We'll all go to the airport with you."

"No, no. I don't want that. Please." Arielle just wanted to be by herself.

The flight back through the late fall rain and snow was rough. Arielle wasn't sure that the pilot could land through the snow and strong northeast winds when they got to Green Star. The pilot, a woman not more than five or six years older than Arielle, approached to within a few hundreds metres of the airstrip, but pulled up when the small plane began pitching back and forth like a wild horse. She circled the community and tried again but passed. On her third approach, a young fellow yelled out from the back of the plane, "You can do it, girl. Put 'er down on the ground. We know you can do it." When the passengers turned to look at him, he gave them a smiling thumbs-up.

Finally, the pilot made another attempt to land, and the plane slammed onto the runway, banging up and down the first couple of hundred metres. When the pilot finally straightened out the plane, Arielle realized how tightly she was gripping the armrest. A cheer went up from the six people on board. Arielle knew it was a matter of pride for young pilots to land their planes in the isolated, northern communities where people were so dependent on the flights. That rough landing reminded Arielle of her own life during the past few days.

She was met at the airport by her grandfather, the chief and a few band councilors. Her grandfather tried to get her to stay at his house, but Arielle insisted on going home. The hardest thing was entering the house. She sat down at the kitchen table where she and her dad had spent so many days talking, laughing and arguing. She looked around the house, seeing all the photos and reminders of her father and mother, feeling the emptiness and remoteness. She stared at the walls, at one of her dad's fishing nets draped over a chair, at his hunting rifle in the corner.

And she felt the silence—complete, cold, airless silence, as if something had been sucked out of the house, all its spirit and energy.

Several elders and community members came that evening to sit with Arielle and talk about her father. They told her how much they had admired him. Arielle knew she would have to be very strong during the ceremony, even with the support of the community. She was on her own now. Completely.

The day after the funeral, she went to the band office to see the band manager.

"I'd like to go out on tomorrow's flight," she told him.

"You sure you want to leave so quickly, Arielle?"

When she didn't answer, he said, "It will be ready innmorning."

Arielle had realized she couldn't stay at the house any longer, even though her grandfather tried to persuade her to stay a few days. It was time to get on with her life as soon as possible.

Arielle's room-mates prepared a big supper for her when she arrived back at the house. They put Arielle to bed when she fell asleep on the sofa at midnight. She refused to talk about her dad, her mom or Green Star Lake, and they stopped expecting that she would.

Bruce and Theresa visited and tried to take her out on those first days back, but Arielle showed little interest. She knew she had to dig deep for the strength that had always got her through on her own. That strength had always been there. This time it was going to be different.

Bruce tried to keep up his relationship with Arielle, but after living in Winnipeg for a month, he sensed that she was not interested in spending time with him. Maybe it was because she had to catch up at school, or maybe it was because her life was busy, but there was definitely a distance growing between them.

He couldn't get the loss of the baby out of his mind. If only that had not happened, they would still be together. Without Arielle in his life, Bruce felt that something had been taken from him, as if he had lost his direction. After six weeks at school, he was bored and not enjoying his courses, and by the end of October was starting to miss his classes. Living at home again was a drag after the freedom he had in Green Star Lake. He was beginning to miss the north. Up there life seemed so real, so immediate, so physically present and so clear. Now his life was a confusing set of signs.

In the first week of November, Bruce got his passport and told his parents he was going travelling. This time, his mother didn't argue or get upset. Seeing the change in her son after he'd come out of the north, she had to let him follow his own path, whether she liked it or not.

Bruce's parents took him to the airport and watched as their confused son headed through the gate to board the plane for Europe. His dad thought that maybe he'd find the direction he sought, after finding some of the answers in Green Star Lake. His mother wondered how things would have turned out if she had not been opposed to Arielle's coming to live with them. It was a question she had to shut out of her mind now. She'd never know.

As the 320 passengers got airborne, Bruce thought about the times he had taken the flight in and out of Green Star Lake on the 10-seater plane that would roar and whine to get into the air. Now the two jet engines whistled them into a steep climb. So different, just as Europe and Green Star would be. Bruce thought about the picnic on the lake in the last week of June, the day before Jimmy was arrested. All of them together, talking, singing, fishing, cooking over an open fire and enjoying the first day of summer. It seemed like a movie he'd seen, but it was real and beautiful. As the jet cruised at 34,000 feet, he thought that maybe he could forget about Arielle for a while.

CHAPTER 8

Vincent

A few days after Jimmy's return from the bush he ran into Vincent at the store. Vincent looked in rough shape. His hair, which had not been trimmed, hung down around his shoulders in greasy clumps. He had lost a lot of weight. His vacant, hollow eyes startled Jimmy. He had never been close to his gay friend, although Vincent had tried hard for over a year to get Jimmy to accept him and become part of his life. Slowly, Jimmy accepted that Vincent was different from other young men, but down deep was reluctant to believe that this difference was normal.

"Hi, Vincent."

Vincent stared at him without answering. Jimmy's first thought was to walk away.

"You okay?" Jimmy asked.

"What difference to you?" Vincent asked and began to walk away.

"Hey, wait, Vincent. What's wrong?"

"Nothing. What's wrong with you?"

Jimmy saw the anger in his eyes. He remembered Vincent as the upbeat, neat, colourful, positive singer, but now he found it difficult to look at the change. Before Jimmy could say anything more, Vincent turned and walked out of the store.

The next evening, Jimmy saw Vincent coming out of the bush.

"Where you headed?" Jimmy asked.

Vincent ignored him and kept walking.

"Hey, wait, Vincent."

Vincent gave him an angry wave without stopping. Jimmy caught up with him and held him by the arm. "Why don't you come over to my place for a cup of coffee?"

"Leave me alone. Aren't you afraid somebody will see you talking to me?" Vincent spat out.

Jimmy was torn between anger and concern for Vincent. He would be more than happy to walk away from this situation, but he took Vincent by the elbow and started in the direction of home.

Inside Jimmy's house, Vincent slumped into a chair while Jimmy's grandmother put a cup of tea on the table. She immediately caught the telltale odour of gas, alcohol and smoke mixing together in the kitchen, that aroma that she had come to associate with Jimmy in the past. She watched Vincent trying to keep his eyes open as he stared at one spot on the table. He was completely silent. She put her arms around him.

"Are you okay, Vincent?"

He said nothing. When his head flopped over the back of the chair, she saw tears slowly rolling down his cheeks. She looked over at her grandson, with his muscular arms, bright eyes and tight skin from his time in the bush, and she looked at Vincent, who was stretched out with his feet under the table, his head now fallen on his chest and arms dangling beside the chair, looking helpless. Lifeless.

Jimmy's grandmother wanted to wash Vincent's hair and give it a good brushing. Those long, braided locks with the blond tips had been his trademark. She put her hand on top of

Vincent's head, stroked it softly and looked at Jimmy with an expectant expression, as if she was waiting for him to do something. Jimmy shrugged his shoulders. He wasn't a doctor or a counsellor, both of which Vincent obviously needed.

They talked as if Vincent wasn't in the room.

"He's been on the juice, for sure. For a while I think," Jimmy muttered. He was beginning to ask himself why he'd brought Vincent home. Jimmy had seen it all too often, and felt there was nothing anybody could do. All he could think of was his friend Gary, who had committed suicide. Vincent was looking and acting just like Gary, and Jimmy didn't want to be reminded of Gary. The last thing he wanted was to get close to anyone who might end his own life. Yet, watching Vincent passed out in the chair, Jimmy felt pulled in two directions, as he often did with Vincent.

"Come on," his grandmother said. "Let's get him up."

Jimmy reluctantly got up, put his arms under Vincent's shoulders and took him over to the sofa.

"Take him to your room, Jimmy," his grandmother said in Cree.

When Jimmy got back to the kitchen she was staring at her cup. "Sad, so sad."

Jimmy didn't respond.

Several minutes passed without any words being spoken. A couple of times, Jimmy caught his grandmother looking at him silently. Finally he asked in Cree, "What?"

"You know."

"No, I don't."

Jimmy asked her again, but his grandmother ignored him, as she had always done in the past when she was showing her impatience. She'd lose herself in her cooking, cleaning or beadwork and go to a place where Jimmy couldn't reach her, a place where she would leave him to deal with the unspoken questions and answers hanging in the air. Jimmy didn't like those times. She had made a point and left him with it.

Jimmy got up and walked down to the dock, where he had gone so many times when he was thinking things over. Jimmy slept on the sofa that night, and Vincent didn't get up until the next evening, but by then Jimmy had left the house. Vincent apologized and hurried shakily out the door.

"Stay, Vincent," Jimmy's grandmother said. "Have something to eat. Wait 'till Jimmy comes home."

"No, no. Thank you. I've got to get going." Vincent needed to find something to get his body and mind in gear. Anything. Some orange-juice brew, a rag of gas over his nose. Now. He disappeared.

When Jimmy got home, and saw that Vincent was gone, he was both relieved and worried. The same old conflict was going on in his head.

"Where did he go?" he asked his grandmother.

She just raised her arms in the air as if to say, "No idea." She still wasn't going to talk about Vincent. When they finished eating, she walked behind Jimmy and squeezed his shoulders as a way to let him know she'd always be there for him. Jimmy went to his room and put on some music. One of the songs reminded Jimmy of the concert Vincent had put on almost a year ago. He remembered how full of life and enthusiasm Vincent had been that night, when he'd led the band in front of the community. The change was like night and day.

Jimmy got up, put on his boots and banged out the door after giving his grandmother a frustrated look. She had a tiny smile on her face. It irritated him.

He went around the community looking for Vincent. Vincent's mother told Jimmy, "I hardly see him anymore. I don't know where he stays and what he's doing, but I know he's not eating." Jimmy knew she couldn't bring herself to talk about everything Vincent was putting into his body.

"It's like he fell off a cliff," she said. "I don't know what to do. And he says nothing when I talk to him. Just stares at me like I'm not even here."

"Is he still doing music?"

"No, not really. He hardly picks up the guitar, and he's usually mad when he finishes playing. Do you know what's happening?"

Jimmy remembered the days when he used to sit and stare like a zombie, living in his world of escape. How could he explain that to Vincent's mother?

"If I find him, I'll let you know," he said to her.

He finally found Vincent the next morning, sitting by himself, leaning against the wall behind the store. His face was turned toward the sun, and he was smiling happily. Jimmy bent down in front of him in the thin layer of early snow.

"Hey, Vincent. Wake up. You okay?"

Vincent opened one eye. "Why would you give a shit?"

"Come on. Get up. It's getting cold. You're going to freeze here." The day had turned much colder now that winter was approaching.

Vincent ignored him.

"Let's go get a coffee."

"Leave me alone." He closed his eyes again.

Jimmy was getting angry. After trying to talk to Vincent for a few minutes, he got up to leave. He heard Vincent say, "So long, asshole. Leave. You're good at that."

Jimmy whirled around with the urge to yell at Vincent, but the picture of Paul talking to him in the bush two months ago came to him. "Get up," he said impatiently, "I'm telling you. Get up!" Jimmy's voice began to rise.

"Naw. I'm okay here."

Jimmy grabbed his arm and yanked Vincent to his feet.

"Let's go."

Vincent didn't fight it. He walked Vincent home. When they arrived, his relieved mother indicated to Vincent's father that they should go outside.

Jimmy sat with Vincent and waited for him to say something—anything.

"It's like living in a black space with no light at all, Jimmy, as if I can't touch anything real. And I can't get up and walk toward anything because I don't know which way to go. I just want to sit and look at the blackness. Let it keep me a prisoner."

It was hard for Jimmy to understand. There had been times when he had been down, especially after Gary's suicide, but his anger usually won out over any other emotion. His everpresent anger was the constant in his life.

He didn't know what to say to Vincent. They sat in silence until Vincent got up and went to his room. Jimmy was about to leave when Vincent's parents came back into the house.

"Stay for supper, Jimmy."

Vincent's mother and father didn't talk much about Vincent. Instead they preferred to ask Jimmy about his time in the bush as a way of dealing with the tension and worry over their son.

When Jimmy left, she said to Vincent's father, "That's what you should do."

"What?" he asked.

"Take him to the bush."

"But he doesn't like hunting. He hates rifles. You know that. What good is it going to do?"

"So take him with his guitar."

"Take him with his guitar. In the boat, with my rifle and fishing gear? Into the bush?"

She didn't give up. "Why not?"

The next day, when his father told Vincent what he wanted to do, Vincent just shook his head. After a short discussion, his father said, "You get ready to go in a few hours."

Vincent knew that the talking was over. It was a "get ready to get in the boat or get ready to pack your things." His mother didn't say a word, and when Vincent turned to her, she told him, "I'm staying out of this."

Later that morning, Vincent trudged down to the dock with his stuff and waited in the boat. He stared across the lake through soft flakes of snow. He was dreading the next few days. He watched his dad come down the hill toward the dock with his gear and Vincent's guitar. Before his father could get in the boat,

Vincent challenged him. "What's with the guitar?"

"Never mind. Start it up. Let's go." Then his dad pointed to the direction he wanted Vincent to go.

Vincent opened the 30-horsepower to three quarter-speed and pointed the boat north. He felt the snowflakes hitting his face like soft needles.

Theresa phoned Arielle several times before getting a call back. It was a couple of weeks after Arielle had returned from Green Star, and Theresa was anxious to know how she was doing.

When they finally got together, Theresa tried to be upbeat and positive, but she found Arielle hard to talk to, and distant. The easy, comfortable relationship they used to have back home was slowly disappearing. She sensed not only sadness but anger in Arielle's mood.

"So have you heard from Bruce?" Theresa asked.

"Yeah, a couple of postcards from him. The last one was from Italy. Some place called Tuscany."

It was as if Arielle could care less.

"So how is he?"

"Hard to tell from a postcard, Theresa."

Theresa pressed on, even though she sensed the tension in

the air and Arielle's irritation.

"Do you miss him?"

Arielle gave a short laugh. "Oh yeah, big time, Theresa."

Theresa knew she was being sarcastic. Theresa got the idea that Arielle was less than interested in talking to her, and after several minutes of trying to reach her friend, she was out of words. Arielle recognized the empty feeling between them and asked Theresa with little enthusiasm, "So how are you doing at school?"

Theresa was becoming upset but tried to keep it going. "School's pretty good." When the conversation turned to Natasha,

Theresa talked excitedly about the baby, but she noticed that Arielle was staring coldly off into the distance, a sign that made Theresa quickly change the subject.

Theresa was glad when two guys came over to the table to talk to Arielle. They wore bandanas and First Nations power T-shirts. Arielle's face brightened, and Theresa saw a quick surge in her friend's energy and talkativeness.

"I'm going to go, Theresa." Arielle gave Theresa a forced smile and began to leave.

"Wait, wait Arielle."

"What?" But Theresa didn't know what to say. She didn't want it to end this way, but Arielle went with her friends, leaving Theresa sitting alone at the table missing the other Arielle. Theresa realized Arielle wasn't going to be the person she used to be, but why did she seem mad at her? Theresa couldn't understand it all at that moment. It would take a little while to figure out what that was all about.

CHAPTER 9

Keith and Natasha

At the beginning of December, Keith contacted her again. He asked about Natasha and her school, but when Theresa asked about his friends, his school and his life, Keith continually changed the subject back to her and the baby. It was only the third time he had spoken to her since she had arrived back in Winnipeg for school. Theresa saw this as an advantage and a disadvantage. On the one hand, she was still connected to him in a way beyond their baby, but she was also happy she didn't have to deal with pressure from him about Natasha.

"I want to apologize for getting so upset about Natasha," he said.

"You already apologized. I understand why you were upset."

"Yeah, but I could have been there more for you, instead of arguing."

"Well, that's over now."

He asked to meet her that week. When they were together, Keith asked if Theresa's mother would come down with Natasha so he could take the baby back to meet his family.

"I've got to think about this, Keith."

"We'll pay for everything, Theresa."

"I don't know, Keith. Give me a couple of days to think

about it. Okay?"

"Sure. Remember my mother brought up six of us. She's great with all the grandkids."

"I'll talk to mom, and I'll phone you on Friday." He understood and didn't pressure her.

On Friday she phoned him. "Okay, mom will do it, as long as there are no complications, Keith."

"Great." She heard the joy in his voice. "When?"

They agreed on the middle of December. "Then all of you can fly back together at the beginning of the Christmas break."

Theresa liked the idea of the three of them going back on the plane at Christmas.

"No surprises, Keith."

"What do you mean, surprises?"

"You know what I mean. No pressure, no surprises and no arguments. My mother doesn't need that."

Keith and Theresa agreed that he and his sister would pick the baby up on Friday and be back to Winnipeg on Monday evening.

Keith did not keep his word. By Tuesday afternoon Theresa had heard nothing.

Theresa phoned Keith's number several times but there was no answer. Finally, on Wednesday, Keith answered the phone and told Theresa, "I think it would be better if Natasha lived with us for a while."

Theresa immediately panicked and yelled at him, "You promised! You promised! You liar. I know I shouldn't have trusted you."

"Calm down, it'll be until after Christmas. It's not going to be permanent."

She continued to argue and yell, but Keith was at his cool best, trying to calm her down and get his way.

"You're going to see, " Theresa shouted. "You'll find out

you're not going to talk and bullshit me into getting your way! Not this time."

She banged down the phone. Her mother put her arms around her. "Just take it easy, Theresa. We'll figure out what to do."

"I'm phoning the RCMP. Right now."

Theresa phoned Beatrice a couple of hours later. "What can I do, Beatrice?"

They discussed all the possibilities, but Theresa had only one thing on her mind. "I want to go up there tomorrow. First thing in the morning. Will you drive me?"

Beatrice could picture the confrontation, the arguing and the chance that things would only get worse. She pictured Theresa up at Keith's home community, trying to get her baby back. Not a good idea. Common sense, intuition and experience told Beatrice that Theresa's plan was not the route to go. "I'll phone you in the morning," Beatrice told her. "Let me talk to your mother."

"I want to know now. If you don't want to do it, I'll get someone else."

Her mother spoke to Beatrice for a minute before asking Theresa to go for a walk. Theresa reluctantly left.

The next morning, Theresa's mother was gone. She left a note for Theresa: "I'll talk to you later. Don't do anything until you hear from me. Listen to your mother. Remember. Wait until you hear from me."

Theresa was unable to contact Beatrice during the day. She accepted that she would have to wait until she heard from her mother.

"I bet she's gone to see Beatrice," Theresa told Susan, the woman who owned the house where she boarded in Winnipeg.

"I hope so."

"I'd say your mother is headed north. Don't the grandmothers usually sort these things out up north?" Theresa thought about that possibility.

"They'll know the right thing to do," Susan said. "Better than you and Keith getting into it again and nothing being settled." Theresa knew she was right.

At supper, she heard her daughter coming through the door. It had all been worked out between the two kookums. Even though Keith had tried to argue that Natasha should stay with them, his mother reminded him that he had made a promise. He wasn't going to have his way. His mother knew what was right and what was best for Natasha. Finally he agreed.

"You're going to have to find a way for Natasha to spend time with Keith and his family, Theresa," her mother told her. "But I can't trust him."

"You let me and his mother worry about that. You two better start thinking about what's best for all of you."

"I'm too mad at him. He'll probably do it again, and next time he might take Natasha someplace else. Hide."

"I don't think so. Keith might be unpredictable, but he loves Natasha too, and he's not going to do anything to hurt her. He wants to be able to see her grow, too."

Two days later Theresa wrote her last test before Christmas. While she was waiting for the flight at the airport with Natasha and her mother, Keith came through the door. He gave Theresa and her mother a hug and took Natasha in his arms.

"She's beautiful, isn't she, Theresa?" "Yes, she is. Just look at those eyes."

"Have a good holiday, Theresa. If there's anything you need when you get back, phone me. Will you do that?"

"Sure, Keith." She smiled at him. This was the Keith she sometimes knew—helpful, understanding and reliable. She also knew the other Keith was always just around the corner.

The word was out in the community that Zach had been

picked up by the RCMP and questioned about the recent series of break-ins and thefts. Things had been quiet in the community. Drug use seemed down, as was the number of things being stolen. It was the quietest that Fred had seen since becoming a band constable. Chief and council had made their point with Jimmy's sentence. It was time to stop the drugs coming into the community. There was no doubt it was a constant struggle, and Jimmy's activities had been a big part of that struggle.

Fred sat across the table from Zach.

"This has got to stop, Zach."

"You guys are blaming everything on me," Zach shot back.

"We know it's you, Zach. What are you trying to prove? It seems that you are breaking in just to break in. I hear you've been suspended from school until after Christmas."

"So what?"

"You tried to get suspended, and now you're happy," Fred told him.

Zach kept up his tough silence. He'd heard that was what Jimmy always did.

"You keep it up, and it's going to be juvenile detention." Zach smiled. Why not, he thought to himself. Jimmy spent 3 months in Juvie. What was the big deal about going to Juvie?

"Can I go now?" he asked Fred.

"Yes, but we're going to talk to your mother and father. Make sure you're home by eleven at the latest."

"Shit." Zach got up and left. There was no way he was going to take that. What could anybody do if he came home later?

When he walked out of the police office, he saw Tracy, a girl from school, waiting for him across the road. He ignored her and headed toward the store, but she caught up with him. What did she want? Ever since the police had picked him up, Tracy had started talking to him. She was in grade 10 and was the best student in her class. Zach was in grade 10 and a poor student. Tracy was popular with everybody. Zach had no friends. Tracy was always in a good mood. Zach seemed to always be in a black mood. Tracy wore bright clothes. Zach wore black. Tracy was one of the first at school and loved talking to everybody. Zach was often late and talked to no one. Tracy liked to joke around with the other students and the staff. Zach seldom smiled. Tracy was tall. Zach was short, at least two inches shorter than Tracy. The only thing they had in common was that they were often in trouble.

Zach wanted nothing to do with her. He seriously doubted that she was interested in him for any reason except for using him in some kind of new get together idea—as if he was going to be someone to test. When he told her he wanted to be by himself, she just kept walking beside him, talking to him, waiting for a response. But Zach didn't trust her. He knew she liked to have fun with people and test them, especially the principal, who found her both smart and surprising. Zach remembered the time she came to school with plenty of make-up and an ultratight outfit that showed too much skin around her waist. It was her way of making a statement about wanting to make her own choices. The principal asked her to cool it on the glamour. She argued and joked with him, and he smiled back at her. "I'll try, but these seem pretty good to me." The principal just looked out the window and shook his head, knowing better than to get into an argument. Tracy knew the power of charm. Nobody got mad at her no matter how irritating she could be. She went home at lunch, changed and toned it down slightly, but spent the rest of that day asserting her right to dress in what she believed was acceptable clothing.

Zach, on the other hand had no charm, and no way with words. He'd only respond with silence. Tracy had watched him and saw it as a challenge. Why? She wasn't quite sure, but she was drawn to his cold, black, silent, skinny, angry personality.

Everything she wasn't. It puzzled her friends when they began to notice.

"You coming back to school, Zach?"

Zach kept walking and tried to shut out the whiff of a beautiful scent coming off her. He looked up at her, trying to figure out where the aroma could be coming from, but refused to talk.

"I'm going to get you to talk to me, Zach. You're not going to ignore me forever." She put her hand on his shoulder as she said it. Zach shook it off.

As they walked beside each other, Zach fought the good feeling that crept over him. By the time they reached the lake, Tracy had taken his hand. His first instinct was to let go, but he felt the electricity go through him. It lasted only a few seconds before he turned on her. "What the hell do you want, Tracy?"

"Nothing, Zach. Why?"

"So why do you keep bugging me?"

"Am I bugging you?" She was wondering herself why she was with him. Taking his hand had made her think a connection had been made. She thought about what her friends would say if they saw her holding his hand but told herself she could not care less.

"Are you bugging me?" Zach repeated. "Are you bugging me? What do you think? Does it look like I'm happy about it?" But Tracy knew it didn't make him unhappy. It was something a girl could tell. She saw it in his eyes, that only time he had looked up at her and knew it wasn't rejection. Tracy was used to getting her way. Zach seldom got his way. When they reached the lake, Tracy took his hand and squeezed it before she turned to go. Zach tried to forget what had just happened, but her aroma and dancing smile stayed. He tried, though.

Vincent didn't speak much during those first days in the bush with his father. He didn't complain but made no effort to pick up the extra 30-30 his dad had hauled into the bush in case Vincent changed his mind. On the fourth day, his father picked up the tracks of a moose. He turned to look at Vincent as if to ask him if he was going to stay in camp or start tracking.

Vincent knew what his father was getting at, even though no words had passed between them.

Later that day, they caught up with the moose. It was standing at the edge of Green Star Lake. They slowly crept to the edge of the clearing. Vincent watched as his father loaded the rifle and quietly knelt behind a rock.

Vincent wanted to turn and look the other way as his dad lined up his first shot, but he couldn't. He had seen this before when he was a young boy, and now he braced himself for what was coming.

Vincent was startled at the noise when the shot rang out in the silence. He couldn't take his eyes off the moose. It stood for what seemed like a long time before it turned to try to escape. His father's second shot brought it down. His dad turned and looked at him. He saw his son standing with a shocked looked on his face. His dad knew at that moment that he could never explain to Vincent how important this way of life was to him, and at the same time it hit him how different his son was from him. So different in their interests and way of looking at things. He felt pain for his son and couldn't help but think that he shouldn't have made Vincent watch. Vincent was also staring at his dad, thinking the same thing.

Both trying to walk toward each other over that awkward gap. "It's better if we let the blood drain out overnight," Vincent's dad said. "It'll be easier to cut up in the morning that way. We'll come back then."

"As long as the lake doesn't start to freeze here in the bay. Can you get the boat in?"

"Should be no problem. By the look of the sky, I think it shouldn't be too cold tonight. It's going to be cloudy and that's not a north wind yet. But who knows in the morning."

On that last night in the bush, Vincent sat in front of the fire with his father and was struggling to stay awake. He wanted to tell his father that he admired him.

"You okay, Vincent?"

"Yeah, I'm okay, Dad."

"You did a good job out there. That was hard for you. I know that you're ready to help. You didn't complain."

"We didn't come so you could listen to me complain." Vincent looked at him.

"I hope you know that it doesn't matter to me that you'll never be a hunter."

"But you'd be happy if I was. Right?" He looked intently at his father. "You're so good at it. It's like you've lived your whole life out there. The way you move through the bush. The way you tracked that moose. I can see how much you love it."

"No, I don't want you to be a hunter. I want you to be good at what you love, Vincent. Not good at what I like doing."

Vincent thought about what his father had told him. When his dad woke up he watched as his son sat by the fire, playing his guitar and singing. He wondered if his son experienced the same thoughts yesterday when Vincent watched as he shot the moose. They and returned to cut up the carcass with the hunting knife he had brought.

"If you don't want to help me cut it up, don't worry about it, Vincent."

"No, Dad. I want to do this." Vincent wanted to do it for his father, but he knew it was the last time he'd ever cut up a moose.

Vincent plowed into the carcass with instructions from his father. "What about the heart and liver, Dad?"

"Those are the favourite parts for some people. And the rump. We'll take all the parts back that can be eaten or used, Vincent."

They loaded the boat and headed back to get the rest of their gear. After making lunch, they put out the fire, loaded everything in the boat and headed for home. The sun was starting to break through the clouds and shine on the perfectly still lake. It bounced off the glassy surface of the water and hit their faces as Vincent's father eased the boat out into the lake. Feeling more at ease now, the two men, father and son, started their journey back, both sensing that the day was going to be warmer than usual for November.

CHAPTER 10

The Race

On the store bulletin board before Christmas, Jimmy saw a poster for a snowmobile race across northern Manitoba for First Nations competitors. Reading the details over, he became excited when he realized this could be a real adventure, not to mention the first place prize of $10,000, as well as several other cash prizes. At first he didn't quite understand how the race would work, but Fred was standing behind him, also reading the poster.

"Pretty interesting, hey, Jimmy?"

"How does it work?"

" Eight hundred miles, ten days of racing, one day of rest in the middle of the race and all those miles through the bush and across rivers and lakes. Pretty good cash prizes, I'd say.

You thinking of entering, Jimmy?"

"Definitely. Why not? I could sure use the cash."

"Everybody north of Lake Winnipeg will be coming up for this one. And probably lots of guys from the south. Look at that.second place is $5,000, and a bunch of other cash prizes."

"Yeah, I understand the cash, but how do they figure out who wins a race over eight days?"

"Every day you go from one point to another. See here on

the map. The race is starting at this red dot, and this shows the route and the next stop at the end of the first day. Everybody starts together, on every day. Then they take your time for each day and add them together and the guy with the lowest total time for all eight days is the winner. So it doesn't matter if you win one day. You've got to be the best overall. Understand?"

"I get it, Fred. You thinking of entering?"

"Thinking about it," Fred answered.

"Hell, you've got one of the fastest Polaris machines around."

"It's not just the fastest machine that's going to win, but the most reliable and the smartest guy who can figure out the easiest and fastest route and the weather. That used Thundercat you bought last year from Richard is pretty fast. You traded your other Arctic Cat for it, didn't you?"

"Yeah, and some cash, of course." Jimmy thought back to last winter when he had the cash and was looking for a faster machine to make it in and out of Thompson. The Thundercat was only two years newer than his last Arctic Cat but had a bigger two-cycle 1000 c.c. in it. He knew it was reliable and fast, and he knew how to do basic repairs in the bush if necessary. He'd learned that he had no choice if he wanted to keep going during those long days. He had already replaced two drive belts in the bush.

Fred looked at him. "Yeah, I heard you had to give Richard some cash. I guess we know where that cash came from. Don't we, Jimmy?" Fred gave him a good stare.

Jimmy ignored the comment, and when he asked Fred if everybody had to follow a certain route, Fred didn't dwell on the subject of last year's cash.

"No way, Jimmy. That's the point of the race—finding the fastest and quickest way between the start and finish each day. That's not going to be easy. Looks easy on the map, but there's a lot of bush and ice out there. You know that."

"Yeah, and the weather."

"Starts the second week of January. This isn't going to be a ride in the spring sun." Fred could see that Jimmy was hooked on the idea. His eyes lit up as he continued to discuss the race. It had everything that appealed to Jimmy—speed, survival, adventure and danger.

"I'm going to do it. And I'm going to win some money. It'll be fun, Fred."

"Maybe, maybe not, Jimmy. Remember you have to bring all your own supplies. You get gas, breakfast and a feast on the fifth day, which is a rest day. You can get all the gas you need in fuel cans. It's free." Jimmy managed to talk the fire chief into letting him put his machine in the fire station so he could work on it. He pulled it off to one side at the back of the building and started to take off some parts. The volunteer firemen from the community got a kick out of seeing him hunched over his beloved Thundercat, cleaning and inspecting all the parts he could get at without extra tools. When the firemen came in the day before the Jimmy planned to take it out on the lake for a high-speed trial, they saw he had painted "Northern Lightning" in bright green letters across the side of his dark blue machine. They were the colours of the northern lights on a cold, blue, winter night. They all gave him a cheer.

During the Christmas break, Theresa arrived home with Natasha and her mother. When she walked down the stairs from the plane, she saw Chance running across the tarmac toward them. Her father was running after him and calling for him to come back, but there was no stopping her son. Reaching his mother, Chance wrapped his arms tightly around her legs and wouldn't let go. When Theresa got home, she lay on her bed with Natasha and Chance on top of her. Theresa and Chance fell asleep with their arms around Natasha, who lay there silently with her wide eyes darting around the room as if she was trying to understand it all.

Theresa spent most of her days with Chance and Natasha. She rarely went out of the house and was glad when Jimmy visited. She got to talk to him about the upcoming big race and watch him play and talk with his son. It was relaxing for her. On Christmas day, Vincent and Jimmy came over with gifts, and the three had a chance to sit and talk about the last three months.

"I don't know what's happened to Arielle," Theresa said. "She seems to have new friends and doesn't have much time for me. I've stopped phoning her. It's like she wants to forget about the past. I can't figure it out."

"She's not a hundred per cent. Been through a lot in the last year," Vincent said. "Maybe she just wants some space for herself. Don't start giving her the dog's eye."

"But we used to be good friends," Theresa complained.

"Ah, we all have our shitty times, Theresa." Jimmy said. "Look at Vincent here. You should have seen him back in October. Looked like some down-and-out bum on the streets. Look at me five months ago—I was sitting in jail. And you were pregnant, worrying about the baby. What happened with her and Bruce? We heard from Lucas he quit school. Is that right?"

"He went to Europe," Theresa said, "I got a couple of post cards from him. I think he's just trying to get away from Winnipeg and thinking about Arielle. She won't even talk about him. I don't know if she's mad at him or doesn't care."

"That's a change for him," Vincent said. "Quitting school. It was always so important to him."

"Well, I always said you never knew what that weird white kid was going to do," Jimmy told them.

Theresa turned to Vincent. "So what happened to you, Vincent? Mom told me that you were having a tough time. You look pretty good now. Thinner. You writing music?"

"I just needed a good kick in the ass, Theresa. Yeah, I'm writing again. It seems like a lot of artists need to go through some kind of crisis to clear the spider webs outta their minds."

Jimmy was going to comment on the change in Vincent. His hair was beautifully brushed back, and his colourful clothes were clean. He looked the way he did that first day he walked into class. except Vincent was now about 20 pounds lighter.

"Is it true you're going in a race after Christmas, Jimmy?" Vincent asked.

"Of course. Why not?"

"He's calling his Thundercat 'Northern Lightning'. It matches his wild, electric personality, eh?"

"I heard. I like that name. It's perfect," Vincent told her.

Jimmy changed the subject. "What's with Keith? We heard there's some problem with Natasha. What was going on?"

"We got it straightened out. It's okay now. I haven't seen him too often, Jimmy. I'm too busy at school."

"Sure. But do you still want to be with him? He's a shithead, you know."

Theresa wasn't interested in getting into a discussion about Keith. She knew how Jimmy felt and wanted to ask him why Keith mattered, but she knew it would only get him started. She just wanted to leave for school in a few days with good feelings between her and Jimmy.

Vincent stepped in quickly. "That's going to be a tough race, Jimmy. Is your machine up to it?"

Jimmy knew that Vincent was trying to change the subject and decided that it was best to let the Keith thing go. It was Christmas.

Jimmy didn't come to the airport when Theresa left for Winnipeg two days later. She told herself he was probably preparing himself for the race, but couldn't deny she was disappointed that he might be still stewing about Keith. Jimmy had always been quick at seeing through what people were thinking, and maybe he was able to figure out that Theresa was still carrying the torch for Keith. If someone had asked her, she would find it hard to say otherwise.

The evening before the race, Jimmy and his grandmother started to pack his suppers for the race. The competitors were expected to bring their own food for seven suppers. They were going to be provided with a feast on the fifth day for those who remained in the race. Jimmy's grandmother planned his food, making sure it was packed as efficiently as possible. Fitting everything on his Arctic Cat was going to take a lot of planning, and now he could see that the race organizers had set up the race so that the entries had things to consider other than just speed. Survival, planning and maintenance of their machines would be just as important.

When they lined up for the start of the first leg of the race on the lake, there were 231 snowmobiles spread across the ice as far as the eye could see. Jimmy was amazed at the variety of machines, some of which he had never heard of or seen. Many were painted especially for the race, with a mixture of hand-painted and professionally designed markings. It was impressive to sit there, listening to the racers winding up their machines while they waited for the local band constable to fire the pistol he had pointed in the air. A woman in traditional dress stood with a First Nations flag that would be pointed in direction of the race when the shot went off

Because many of the racers were anxious to get going, several of them took off at top speed and spread out in a "V" around the two figures who had signalled the start of the big competition. While several of the racers took big leads in the first half-hour, many of them decided to start the first leg of the race at a medium pace, knowing that the day and the distance were going to be long, and there was no rush. There was no point in pushing it right from the start. When Jimmy looked back, he saw that a few machines were still on the starting line, with men leaning over them, trying to figure out what was wrong.

Jimmy told himself, "Be cool, be relaxed. Be there at the end." It was something he was going to repeat over and over again during the coming days.

Jimmy felt for the small leather bag he kept in the inside pocket of his snowmobile suit. Paul had come to him with a small package, as he had when Jimmy was in the bush. "You might need these in six or seven days. They are different from the ones I gave you that day I met you up north."

After studying the map all the racers had been given, Jimmy saw that the route of the first day was going to be straightforward: 130 miles.

Half-way through the first day, the pace began to pick up as racers in the middle of the pack, and those near the end of the long stream of snowmobiles, pushed to get closer to the front. Jimmy opened his machine to 90 per cent power, and he started to pass other machines. The weather was still quite nice for January, partially sunny and little wind. He undid the top of his snowmobile suit and shifted from side to side to relax his body. When he pulled into the first stop at the end of the day, he learned he was 27 minutes behind the leader, a guy running a bright yellow Polaris with the names of his children on the side in purple letters. Jimmy smiled when he caught sight of the Polaris. The colours reminded him of Vincent's clothes. Several fires were quickly started and groups of men began to gather around the warmth with their sleeping bags. Listening to the other six racers around the flames, he learned that 22 racers had already dropped out. A couple had tried to take a short cut across a long stretch of bush and had to be rescued by the helicopter provided by the race organizers. It was too easy to get far off course, or worse, break down in the vast wilderness. Jimmy found it amusing that a helicopter would be needed for guys who lived in the north, but learned that one had been injured and lifted out by helicopter from a location where it might have been impossible to find or reach him.

It wasn't long after the meal that everybody began to crawl into sleeping bags beside the fires The race organizers had decided that they would be provided to keep the fires going through the night so everybody could get a good night's sleep. When Jimmy pulled his sleeping bag around him and settled in, he began to realize how sore and stiff his body was. He could still feel the vibrations of his machine.

On hearing the horn go off at seven o'clock in the morning, Jimmy rose to eat the food the organizers had provided—eggs, bannock and jam, fruit, bacon and coffee. Lots of coffee. Walking toward his Thundercat, Jimmy noticed several competitors working over their snowmobiles. At eight o'clock, everybody was placed in a line according to their recorded times from the previous day. It took a while for the racers to get used to the system, since they had just grouped together on the lake the previous day. But on the second morning, the race was going to start in the bush, and it was impossible to have everybody in one group at the start. The race organizers explained that this was the way it was going to be on the mornings they weren't starting on a lake, so it was important to finish as high as possible to get a good starting spot the next morning. Jimmy knew that there were so many lakes that they could easily begin each day on the ice, but he figured the line-up system was another planned challenge. He understood this immediately, since his starting position was number 67 on the second day, and he wasn't able to get going until a few minutes after the first racer left.

By the fourth day, there were only 128 racers left. The rest had quit, some of them because their machines had broken down. The second and third days had been relatively uneventful. The weather had stayed clear and quite warm for January, allowing the racers to find their way across the lakes and rivers and through the bush. While some people had pushed on at terrific speeds to try to gain a large time advantage that might discourage others, Jimmy had made his mind to stay in the top 45. With five days of racing to go, he knew there were still many things that could go wrong for everybody. What was the point of pushing his machine at top speed and risking a mechanical problem or breakdown when the end was not in sight?

In the evenings, Jimmy was getting to know some of the others. Before hitting their sleeping bags they would talk about what had happened to them or what they had seen during the race. Some of the stories were funny; others were about machines coming to a stop; and one was about two snowmobiles colliding as they raced to the finish line on the third day.

"Yeah, it was pretty amazing," one of the racers told the group. "These two guys came around that last turn, you know where there's that last bunch of trees about a quarter-mile from the end. So these two guys come to the end of the turn, and they're both trying to get out first on that straight part, like two stock cars coming out of the pits. You know, jockeying for position. One of the guys manages to get in front and all of a sudden he slows down. The guy behind him still has it wound up to full speed and climbs all over the back of the guy in front."

He stops and demonstrated with his hands how the trailing machine rode over the back end of the other and over on its side. "So you'd think with a couple of hundred yards to go the guy in the front would finish the race. But no. What does he do? He stops his machine, turns around and helps the other guy get going, and they both finish together at the same time."

"So was there any damage?" asked a fellow sitting around

the fire.

"I don't think so. They were both lucky. The whole thing was pretty neat."

"Did you see that black-and-red machine come through the bush and take off from the ledge? The guy probably didn't realize there was a drop and musta been going when he hit the edge. You could just see his head and body come up as he started flying through the air. like he was wondering where he was and what was going to happen."

"So what happened?"

"He hit the snow about eight feet below. You could see his whole body go down on his machine. Like a spring. But I gotta give it to him. He came right outta there and kept going.

Not even slowing down or stopping to check anything."

Everybody seemed to have something to talk about except Jimmy. He sat quietly, enjoying the companionship.

"So Jimmy, how's that two-cycle of yours going? That's a pretty old Cat, isn't it?"

"It's good. No problems yet. Not that old."

"I guess we'll find out the next few days, eh?" The racer asked.

"Yeah, you're definitely going to find out." Jimmy gave him a confident smile.

At the beginning of the eight day, Jimmy was number 19 and 32 minutes behind the leader.

The weather was still warm for January, but there was an increasing northeast wind. There were still short periods of sun, but Jimmy knew from experience that snow was coming. By the end of the day, a light snow had begun to fall, and the skies had darkened with clouds. The leader was a young guy riding a bright orange Yamaha decorated with a painting of a man's head with stars flowing from his hair. Jimmy thought it was the best design in the whole field. In second place was a girl in her early twenties on a brightly coloured Ski-Doo GTX. What else thought Jimmy? Flowers painted on the side. He thought it looked like a garden.

There were lots of comments about the girl—mostly good natured put downs or sarcasm. She visited everybody each night, joking and encouraging the others. When she sat down around the fire with Jimmy's group on the fourth night, he got up and left. He wanted no part of her head games. All he could think about was that it would be hard to swallow if a girl won the race. How could he go back to Green Star and admit it? Yet he had to give her credit. She was in second place, several places in front of him.

One of the competitors Jimmy was getting to know was a guy who had passed him earlier in the day on a black machine with orange flames and the name "Flamethrower" painted on the side. Jimmy laughed when it passed him, but he noticed the guy give him the fist, as if he was mad about something. The young guy came over to him on that night when Jimmy was eating.

"Next time, get out of my way if you want to run your machine like an old man. Stay behind me where you belong, kid."

Jimmy refused to take the bait. Instead, he just looked the guy up and down, as if to say, "Who made you king of the race?"

The next day was a day of rest and for any needed repairs. Most of the racers slept in. After getting something to eat, they began checking their snowmobiles. Parts started to come off. Jimmy heard swearing as they struggled with tools and cold parts. Jimmy looked at his drive belt, which still seemed to be in pretty good condition, but he decided to replace it anyway. Taking no chances, he also took apart the carburetor and checked that it was clean. He had noticed that the Cat was noisier than usual, but he could find no other problems on that day In the late afternoon, the snow picked up while racers were enjoying a feast put on by the race organizers.

Day broke with heavy blowing snow, but the temperatures were still not too cold. Jimmy and a few others sat around the fire and studied the map.

"I think it would be better to go straight through here and across the lake to end of this leg," one said. "It's going to be really tough to see in the open if this snow and wind gets any worse."

"Yeah, that's true, but if you take the bush most of the way, we'd have a better idea of where we are." one man argued.

"You'd get lost out there in the middle of the lake and it's going to be a while before anybody is going to find you." "And run outta gas, too," another racer added.

"Some of us should stick together in a group in case someone has a serious problem. At least nobody will get left in the bush by himself."

"You think they'll cancel the race for today because it's too dangerous?"

"I doubt it. This is part of the challenge. Got to bear down and be a good navigator. It's not going to be speed today."

Another guy nodded. "Just get from here to the next point and hope this blows over."

Jimmy listened and decided that he'd hook up with three or four other racers for the day. He had moved up to 23 in the race, and it would be foolish now to try to pick up a few places by taking too many chances. Five of the racers decided on a plan and left a few minutes after the race started, all taking turns in the lead. At noon, they stopped and checked their maps.

"Seems like a lot of people did the same thing," one said.

"I don't think we need to stick together the rest of the day. I'm going to push it this afternoon."

"What are you going to do, Jimmy?"

"Not sure."

"You don't say much, do you?"

"I figure he's going to do his talking out there," one man said, pointing toward the next few stops.

"I think we've done okay today," Jimmy said. "I'm going to figure how things are when we leave. Not going to decide right now. I'll see you guys at the fire tonight."

Only three people got lost that day. Amazing, Jimmy thought as he sat in front of the fire and looked across at the blowing snow.

To his surprise when he got up in the morning, the snow was gone, and the clouds were beginning to break They had been lucky. Jimmy noticed the temperature had dropped, and the race organizers called everybody together and told them that the forecast was for 31 below at the end of the day. Typical, thought Jimmy. A snowstorm, followed by clear, cold weather. When everybody went to their machines on day seven, several of them had difficulty getting started, but the bright yellow machine with the flowers was up at the starting line as if she was saying,

"Come on, guys. I'm waiting."

Getting extra supplies and snowmobile parts during the race had been prohibited. That was why the end of each leg was not located close to any community. This was part of the survival aspect of the race. Alcohol was also banned from the race, although Jimmy noticed more than a few guys pulling out small containers that morning to ward off the coming cold. The men had probably carried them from the start for such a moment. Jimmy reached into the top pocket of his snowmobile suit and pulled out the small bag Paul had given him. He'd almost forgotten about it, but with three days left in the race, he was curious about the effect the crushed powder would have. At the last moment, he remembered Paul's final words.

"Use this when you really need it. Save it for then."

Jimmy sat on his Cat, letting it warm up and thought about the route for the day. He was now in 24th place out of the 98 competitors who were still in the race. He was 17 minutes behind the leader. Could he make that up in two days? He thought so.

Of the 98 racers left, many were having trouble starting their snowmobiles. Those who could get started helped the others, and all the competitors decided that the race wouldn't start until nine o'clock, to give everybody a chance to get going. Jimmy turned off his Thundercat and walked over to a large fire.

He heard from those standing around the fire that the temperature had dropped to 23 degrees below zero. There was not much joking around the fire as everybody waited for the starting horn to go.

Jimmy studied the map. There were several islands between the starting and the finishing line that day. He tried to decide whether it would be easier to take the longer routes around the islands or to see if a trail was established through the middle of the bush on each island.

As they sat on their machines in the frigid temperatures, Jimmy noticed that it was perfectly still. Not even the slightest breeze. He felt the big breakfast he had eaten, as well as the three cups of black coffee sitting in his stomach.

When the horn went off at nine, three racers were still trying to start their machines. Frozen gas lines, Jimmy thought.

Everybody went off at half-speed as if they were waiting to see what was going to develop.

The day was uneventful. The racers formed a long line for most of the day, as if trying to huddle against the dropping temperatures and make it to the finish line at the end of the day. There were few passes, so the order of racers was still much as it was in the morning. Jimmy moved up three spots but only because five machines just stopped in the middle of the afternoon. The competitors were quickly picked up, although they had to leave their snowmobiles where they stopped since nobody wanted to work on them in the icy temperatures. The machines would be hauled out later.

At the end of the day, the race organizers called everybody together around a giant fire to let them know that the temperature was predicted to hit 31 below by morning.

"We're thinking that this is getting too dangerous if these temperatures don't improve," one organizer said. "We can camp here until things get better or go on. We don't want anyone dying out there. Sure, we wanted this to be a tough challenge, but we can't let it become too dangerous for everybody. We'd like all of you to discuss it. I know some of you want to go on tomorrow, and some are undecided. If we don't get a clear decision from you, we'll decide and let you know. We're trying to be fair to all of you."

The older competitors were leaning toward waiting a day or two, while the younger guys wanted to push on those last two days. The discussion went back and forth until "Flamethrower" spoke up: "What a bunch of chickenshits! I'm disgusted with some of you. Why don't you guys who want to hide out here for summer to come, go home and hide in your beds?"

The talk was over. The vote was to go on the next day. Jimmy was all in favour of continuing. Chickenshit? Oh yeah, just wait, he raged.

When the day started, the race organizers spoke to each competitor and checked on survival supplies. Thirty racers Lined their machines up to the starting line at eight o'clock. Jimmy looked a few hundred yards down the lake and was glad to see the helicopter warming up, spewing out massive clouds of exhaust.

Jimmy studied the map. It looked like a straight shot across several lakes with some bush in between. Not too much to decide about the route. That morning the racers wound up their machines and roared off as if they were anxious to get the day over. The first four or five racers broke trail for a while, and then dropped back a few places to let others in the pack take over the trail-breaking. Jimmy knew that this kind of co-operation couldn't continue forever. This was a race, but he also knew everybody was trying to make sure they could get their snowmobiles to the end of the day without a breakdown.

By the end of the day, only two more racers had dropped out. Jimmy found out he was still 18 minutes behind first place with one day left. After a quick supper, everybody crawled into their sleeping bags, close to the fires. There was little talk and none of the laughter that usually was heard at the end of the day.

That last night, Jimmy slept poorly. He got up in the middle of the night, walked to the edge of the ice and looked across the vast expanse of snow and trees. The stars were brilliant and seemed almost touchable in the blue-black sky. He was exhausted. His body felt sore and stiff, from his ankles to his neck, as though he had been stretched and twisted in a tornado. One day left. He was looking forward to the end. Northern Lightning had been a good machine, even though it was idling roughly and sometimes needed starting again if Jimmy sat too long without accelerating.

But that was minor. He knew the Thundercat would take him to the end.

Jimmy reached into the upper pocket of his snowmobile suit and pulled out Paul's small leather bag. Reaching in with two fingers, he pinched up a good portion of the contents and put it under his tongue for a few minutes, as Paul had instructed, before swallowing all of it. He did that twice.

After sleeping for another hour, Jimmy woke up before the horn went off to start the day. Most of his stiffness and weariness had faded. His appetite was huge at breakfast. There were few words in the morning. Everybody knew that this day was for the money, plain and simple. No traveling in a pack. No holding back and no three quarter-speeds. The organizers told the group that there were 18 racers within 32 minutes of the leader.

"There's still many of you who could be in the money. The good news is that the temperature is up to 28 degrees below." That got some laughs.

"We were looking for a great race and it looks like we've got it. Several of you could still get first or second place. So good luck today."

By the time he mounted the Cat, Jimmy was wide-eyed and full of energy. He still had a little of the mixture in Paul's bag.

The organizers reversed the order on the last day. The last-place-racer started first, and the first started at the end of the line. Jimmy thought this was a good idea; it would make the last leg more competitive.

Everybody went off at maximum power down the lake towards a trail. Within three miles, they hit the lake and fanned out into a widely spread formation of brightly coloured, speeding machines. The men in the helicopter hovered above, marvelling at the sight of rocketing, pitching racers as they plowed through drifts, sometimes flying off small mounds. The helicopter crew was sure there would be several to pick up that last day.

Jimmy had studied the map with care, trying to figure out how he could make up the length of time he was behind. The racers all had a choice—follow a southeasterly route or try to cut across a large island and save time. Jimmy was only interested now in getting into the money, so it was an easy decision, even though he would be taking a big risk. He would go for the shorter route and for the cash. Better to have least tried, even if he dropped down several spots in the order at the end of the race.

By the middle of the day, he was feeling good about his progress. He thought he was by himself, but when he came to a sharp turn, he spotted the Flame Thrower. Jimmy hadn't noticed anybody else taking the turn with him, coming off that last island, and he figured he would be following that route by himself. Obviously Flamethrower had come to the same conclusion about trying to win money, or else he had something to prove to Jimmy. When Jimmy slowed to avoid a fallen tree, the black-and-orange machine closed to within 50 feet of him. Soon he was on Jimmy's tail, pushing to pass. As Jimmy pushed the throttle to pick up speed, he noticed the Flamethrower getting ready to beat him to a narrow opening between an outcropping of rocks and some trees. Both raced to be first through the gap. Jimmy felt a sharp, metallic bang as he refused to yield any room to the other racer. The Flamethrower grazed the edge of the rocks, catching the front of his machine. Jimmy looked back over his shoulder. The black snowmobile rose in the air, and then rolled, heading straight for a spruce tree. The black, hurtling metal hit the spruce, reared up and threw the racer forward, face first, into the trunk of the tree. Jimmy stopped. He idled his Arctic Cat and stared at the wreck and at the rider lying in the snow. He circled back, got off his Thundercat and plowed his way to the injured racer lying in the snow. When Jimmy rubbed snow on his forehead, he began to wake up.

"Come on," Jimmy said. "You've got to get on my machine. Let's go." But when he saw the crooked arm, Jimmy realized that it had been broken, and it would take a major effort to get his rival on the Arctic Cat.

"Naw...naw...no way. Go on. I'll take care of myself," he groaned.

Jimmy couldn't believe that he was having to argue with the man. He continued to reject Jimmy's help.

"Don't be such an asshole. You're going to freeze here in the bush."

"Just help me start a fire."

Jimmy couldn't believe what he was hearing. He walked over to his snowmobile and dumped all his gear in the snow. Then he pulled the injured young man up, walked him to the Arctic Cat and sat him down. Climbing on the Thundercat, Jimmy positioned the broken arm between their bodies and told the racer to hold on as best he could with his good arm.

When Jimmy got to the middle of the next lake, he stopped and waved down the helicopter, which was making a pass over the area, looking for stragglers.

He had the 19th best time overall when he arrived at the finish line. He was out of the money. He wondered where he would have been if the accident hadn't happened.

The racers were all put up in hotels, and very few were awake before the next afternoon.

When everybody met at the dinner that evening for the awarding of prizes, the racers exchanged plenty of stories, slaps on the back and special handshakes. The winner of the $10,000 prize was a 63-year-old racer who had hung back for most of the race, using his experience, knowledge and sense of the northern terrain to find the fastest route on that final leg. The organizers asked him to say a few words. In a soft voice, he said, "Megwetch". Then in Cree, he told the racers to be proud of themselves—they had the spirit of the north for not giving up. In total, 12 cash prizes were awarded. The girl with the bright yellow machine got sixth place. Pretty good, thought Jimmy watching her move through a crowd of racers with a big smile, shaking their hands. Then, several competitors stood up and told their stories to applause and some laughs. Near the end of the dinner, the Flamethrower got up. He told the story of the last couple of hours with Jimmy.

"He might have placed right near the top if he didn't have to stop." Jimmy was embarrassed but not too unhappy about the outcome, when he received a cheque from the race organizers for $1,000 as a special prize.

A couple of weeks after the race, he took the Thundercat out into the middle of the lake and tried to take it to full power. He could feel the machine trying but failing to rev up to its former strength. Like a tired stallion, it needed rest and loving care. He turned for home, and after parking the machine behind his grandmother's house, he lay back on the rumbling 1000 ccs and thought about the race. It felt good.

Theresa got the news about the race from her mother. She sent a letter to Jimmy.

CHAPTER 11

Theresa and Keith

But Theresa was missing one thing—that closeness with somebody, being held in someone's arms. When she fell asleep some nights, she was able to shut out the bad times and fights with Jimmy and remember the way they used to be when they were close and loving, the times when Theresa managed to get past Jimmy's anger and toughness. But those days were gone, and Theresa didn't see them returning. Often her thoughts turned to the days when she and Keith used to spend weekends with each other. Those thoughts prompted her to call him in the middle of February. Although she told him that she'd like to see him so they could talk about Natasha, she knew that she wanted more than a discussion. She ended up spending the weekend going to a dance and a few parties. It was like old times, and she and Keith were two good friends again. But her heart told her one thing, and her head said something else. When Keith dropped Theresa off Sunday evening, she wasn't expecting to hear from him or to see him for a while. What would be the point of asking him to phone, she asked herself? She had made up her mind that the best thing Keith could do was to be a good father to Natasha and a good friend to her. There were going to be times when Keith could make her life easier and be someone she could talk to, but he would probably never be the partner Theresa had always wanted him to be. She had come to accept that, instead of living in a world of unrealistic expectations. When she got to her room, she felt none of the anger and resentment she used to feel about Keith. She fell asleep quickly.

Theresa was shopping one day when she ran into Arielle, who was standing with a young man. Arielle turned around and caught Theresa looking at her from across the store.

Theresa hurried over to Arielle and gave her hug. Arielle seemed uncomfortable.

"Hey, how come you haven't phoned?" Theresa asked.

"I've been really busy, Theresa."

"So you could at least call me back, eh?"

"Yeah, I know. I'm sorry."

Theresa didn't think Arielle was sorry.

"Come on, Arielle. Let's get something to eat."

"Someone's waiting for me."

"Can't you see him later? It's been a long time, Arielle."

"Okay, but I haven't got a lot of time."

It was an upsetting time for both of them. Theresa could tell that Arielle didn't want to be there. Theresa tried to be in a good mood and attempted to get Arielle to talk.

"Have you heard from Bruce?" Theresa asked.

"I got a post card last week from Russia."

"Wow. Russia. How's he doing?"

"It sounded like he was enjoying himself."

"Is he still crazy about you?"

Arielle laughed and ignored Theresa's question.

"I bet he is," Theresa told her.

"Are you seeing Keith?"

Theresa didn't want to talk about Keith, but she told Arielle about the weekend.

Arielle became silent.

"What's the matter, Arielle?"

"You're such a fool. Keith just does whatever he wants, and you're only too happy to go along with it like some faithful puppy."

Theresa was shocked because she hadn't felt like that after the weekend with Keith.

"What's the matter with you, Theresa? Eighteen and already two babies. What's wrong with you? Can't you see where you're going? You'll be twenty-two and land up with four or five babies 'cause you can't quit giving in to the guys in your life."

Theresa didn't know what to say. "What are you talking about? It's not like that..." Arielle cut her off.

"Sure it is, and you know I'm right. You can't even take care of your kids. You're down here and they're up north. What kind of mother is that?"

Theresa was unable to speak. The guilt that was always close to the surface flooded over her.

Arielle kept it up. "What are you going to be? Some woman with a bunch of kids who needs someone to take care of her. What's the matter with you? You're so naive. So blind."

"What?" Theresa began to cry and she could see that Arielle was furious. "Don't, Arielle. Please don't say that."

"What? Tell you the truth? Is that it? I've got to go." Arielle got up.

"Don't go," Theresa pleaded. "Not like this."

But Arielle wasn't listening anymore. "Take care of yourself, Theresa." She was gone.

Theresa sat by herself, staring at the table, unable to move. What had just happened? Theresa was devastated and confused.

When Jimmy's grandmother answered the door she saw Zach pacing in front of the house. "Is Jimmy home?"

"He's sleeping, Zach."

"Oh, okay. I'll come back later."

"No. Come in." She opened the door and waited for him, but he stood still.

"Come on. Come on. It's cold out there." He sauntered in and sat at the kitchen table.

She didn't ask him if he wanted to eat but made a big breakfast and put it in front of him with a cup of coffee. She watched him quickly finishing the meal. As he was about to leave, Jimmy walked into the kitchen.

"Boy, Zach, you're like a detective following me around."

"Just wanted to talk to you about the race."

"Is that all?"

Zach nodded.

"I'm a little tired right now." Jimmy told him.

When it looked as if Zach wasn't about to leave, Jimmy did a quick summary of the race. Zach just nodded, got up and headed for the door.

"You going to school?" Jimmy asked.

"Yeah. Some days."

"You should forget about all those other ideas you had, Zach, you're almost eighteen.

CHAPTER 12

Tracy

When Zach got outside, Tracy was waiting for him and began walking beside him. They had walked only a short distance, when Zach began to feel her body brushing up against him. She took his hand and squeezed it. A half-hour later, they found themselves far out on one of the trails leading out of Green Star Lake. Standing in the snow, Zach stared across the lake, thinking about Jimmy and when he could tell him about his plans. Tracy was standing behind him with her chin resting on top of his shoulder. She wrapped her arms around him and locked her hands together on his chest. Zach stood like a stone statue, unable to move. Tracy rocked him back and forth. Soon she felt Zach's body start to relax and soften. They stood that way for a long time. Zach closed his eyes.

When they turned for home, Zach didn't resist when she took his hand and asked, "You okay, Zach?"

Zach nodded, staring at the ground. A sliver of warmth went through him when she squeezed his hand and leaned over to kiss him on the cheek.

When they arrived back to the community, Tracy told him, "That was nice, Zach." They separated and each headed for home. Trudging down the road, Zach felt the emptiness begin to return. He didn't want to think about the next time he and Tracy would be together again.

Tracy decided she'd visit her best friend before going home. She was tired and wanted to go home to sleep, but she wondered whether her mother and father would still be fighting. When she left the house in the morning, her mother was angry with her father because he had said he was leaving again for a few weeks. Tracy knew that two weeks usually meant a month or more until she'd see her dad again. It was upsetting for Tracy. She never knew when he'd return or if he'd return. Walking by herself, she wondered if her dad had somebody else in the city. Or did he no longer want to be with her mother? Her father, who had always been a quiet, distant man, now seemed to be drifting away from Tracy, and she couldn't figure out how to reach him. It seemed there were days when he wanted to spend time with her; other times he just wanted to be by himself. During those times, Tracy felt rejected, especially when she was younger and looking for a closeness with him that appeared to be out of reach. She had learned to accept the reality and be happy with the times when he was talkative and happy to be at home with his family. But life with him was always up and down, making Tracy unsure of what was coming next. She had made up her mind that if she was unhappy, there were always ways to get herself to feel good. So she had become the most popular, best dressed, smartest student at the school, and also the most attractive. She got the sense that people thought she was a flirt with men, but Tracy didn't have to try to attract men and the boys at school. Visitors to the community often commented that Tracy looked older and more mature than her age. She enjoyed her popularity and used it to her advantage. That led to several boys being under the impression that she was interested in them. That had caused a few arguments and some angry accusations from some of the other girls at school and in the community. Tracy ignored it all. She liked being with the boys at school and the young men in the community more than spending time with girls her age. Although she'd had some boyfriends, the relationships had only lasted a few weeks and never became serious or anything that Tracy wanted to continue. It gave her a good feeling to know that young men wanted to be with her, but nothing changed in her relationship with her father as she grew older and as he spent more time away from home.

She thought about Zach. He was different from the rest because he didn't seem interested in her.

She couldn't figure that out. Tracy wanted to change that and knew that she could.

Jimmy didn't say much when he visited Paul, preferring to watch Paul paint a drum. Paul hadn't asked Jimmy about his vision quest during those months in the bush. Jimmy had dropped in a few times after the race, but talked about things that had nothing to do with the visions he had in the bush or the bag of ground leaves and seeds that Paul had given him for the race. Paul let Jimmy talk about what was on his mind, instead of trying to pressure him to open up about the nights he had spent alone in the bush, when he would have experienced a new awareness of what was possible through the voyages in his mind. Paul was used to this. At times, Jimmy was interested in talking about traditional ideas and knowledge, but on other days, he just sat and watched the shaman craft a creation from materials he found in the natural world around him. One day when Jimmy was leaving, he told Paul, "I'll come back some day and talk about those days in the bush, Paul. I know it's been a while since I was there by myself, so I want to talk to you about what happened in my head. All the things I saw. The pictures and places I visited. I will, Paul."

"When you're ready, Jimmy. No rush."

Jimmy walked home, thinking about the past five months, the days in the bush and the big race. It was all in the past now. Jimmy shifted his thoughts to the future. What next?

He was beginning to feel restless again. He picked up the mail and read the letter from Theresa. He thought about getting on the plane to Winnipeg but quickly forgot about that idea. Instead, he wandered through the front door of the school. It was the first time he had entered the building without having to be there. He walked through the halls and out the back door, knowing he had gone as far as he could with school in Green Star Lake. Now, he'd either have to go out for grade 11 like Theresa or take correspondence courses if he wanted to stay at home.

A few days later Jimmy ran into Vincent, who seemed to be back to his old self. He had the light back in his eyes.

Vincent still wanted to talk about the race. "I still want you to tell me more about the race. About that last day. It must have been tough."

"Ahh, Vincent. That was a while ago. I've mostly forgotten about it."

"Yeah, sure. You always want to lay low." Vincent laughed.

Jimmy was thinking about his walk through the school the day before, not the race, which was now old history for him. Time to move on. Time to figure out his next move. Jimmy's mind was clicking over about the future, not the past.

"You going back to school, Vincent?"

Vincent thought Jimmy was talking about school at Green Star. "Yeah, I go in and teach music and singing Monday, Wednesday and Friday afternoons. They actually pay me for it. You should go in and tell the little kids about your days in the bush. and the race."

"I don't think so." Jimmy laughed. No way, he thought to himself. Besides, Jimmy still didn't want to be seen to be too close to his gay friend, although Vincent's suggestion made him think about why he had walked through the school yesterday afternoon. No, that wasn't in his immediate plans.

"Are you going to get your grade 11?" Vincent asked.

"Don't know."

"You going out?"

"Don't know, Vincent."

"You could even start the last term this spring."

"Nah, too soon. What about you?"

"I'm thinking about going out. You know. Scope things out."

"When?"

"I'm not going to be here next year. That's for sure."

CHAPTER 13

Arielle and Theresa

Beatrice sat across from Theresa, listening to her talk about Arielle.

"She's Arielle's. So tough now."

"So you think she's mad at you?"

"Oh yeah. Told me how stupid I've been."

"Stupid, why stupid?"

"Having two babies, Keith in my life , not taking care of my children, seemed like everything I was doing. Made me feel like a failure."

"Why a failure?"

"Eighteen and two children, not able to separate myself from Keith."

"Hey, hey, Theresa. Stop it."

"Stop what?"

"Feeling guilty. Feeling as if you've done something wrong." Theresa went silent.

"Have you thought about what happened to Arielle?" Beatrice asked.

"You mean losing her baby? Her dad dying? Bruce?"

"Yes. She lost her dad and a baby in five months, and here you are with two healthy babies."

Right away, Theresa saw what Beatrice was getting at. She had been too busy thinking about her own feelings. "Yeah, I see. Of course."

Beatrice nodded.

"Why is she taking it out on me, though?"

Beatrice looked at Theresa as if she should have the answer. "Not really mad at me but my life and what I've got.

Not that my life is so great."

"Yes, Theresa. So quit blaming yourself."

"I get it. I just happen to be someone who reminds her of what she's lost."

"Yep." Beatrice smiled at her.

"But I can't do anything about it, Beatrice."

"No, of course not. All you can do is understand what's going through her head. She probably doesn't see it clearly herself."

"Tough for her to hear me talk about Chance and Natasha."

Before Beatrice dropped her off, Theresa was feeling better about things.

"So should I phone her?"

"Wait for her."

At the spring break, Theresa phoned the education councilor in Green Star Lake and asked if the band would pay for a return ticket to Winnipeg before her last term started. She needed to see Natasha and Chance and connect with people in her community. She also missed her mom and dad, her house, her friends, Jimmy, Vincent and everything that was familiar and comfortable. She didn't have to explain it to the education councilor. He could hear it all in the sound of her voice and knew it was time for her to come home for a break. He didn't want to risk having Theresa quit school with only three months to go.

Three days later, Theresa was on the plane flying north. When she landed in Green Star and walked out of the plane, she caught the smell in the northern air of spring approaching. A spark of energy lifted her spirits. She saw her mom and dad waiting for her, and Chance running toward her. When she picked him up in her arms, she thought about Arielle.

Later in the day Jimmy dropped over. "I didn't think you were coming home until the summer." Jimmy said to her.

"You've got to tell me about the big race."

"No big deal."

She laughed. "No big deal. You're so good at not letting people see what you're thinking and feeling." Jimmy was uncomfortable and started talking to Chance while they all sat around kitchen table. He watched Theresa bottle-feeding Natasha. Keith's baby. Not his. But he had to admire Theresa—her way of getting through anything without anger or resentment, her refusal to give up. He sat watching her, unable to decide whether she was a friend or something more than a friend. It was difficult to sort out after all that had happened.

Theresa could sense the restlessness in Jimmy that she had seen so often in the past, always so close to the surface when he had too much time on his hands and not enough to do, or some challenge to overcome.

"I was talking to Lucas at the store yesterday," Theresa said. "He told me he got a couple of post cards from Bruce."

"Oh yeah. What now?"

"You never liked him, did you?" Theresa asked.

Jimmy didn't answer.

"Anyway, I thought it was pretty good that Bruce sent them to Lucas. He's in Italy now."

"What's the weird white kid doing now? What about him and Arielle?"

"I don't know. I don't see Arielle too much these days."

Jimmy could see the sadness in Theresa's eyes but didn't ask her what had happened. It was for them to sort out. Two girls not getting along meant trouble, thought Jimmy and something to stay away from.

Theresa continued, "I've tried, but she's got into some political stuff with a young crowd at the university. I figure it's best just to let her live her life. Not interfere." She quickly changed the subject. "Why is Zach hanging around your place?" Jimmy shrugged.

Theresa went on. "He's a young guy headed for a lot of trouble from what I hear. When I saw him at the band office, he was just leaning against the wall, staring at everybody. You know, with those beautiful, mysterious dark-purple eyes. Like some kinda character out of a movie. What's he up to?"

"I have no idea." Jimmy threw his hands up in the air as if to say, "Why are you asking me?"

"So what are you going to do? Are you coming to Winnipeg in September for grade 11?" Jimmy shrugged.

"Why not? The band will support you."

"The Chief is going to want to support me in Winnipeg?

Yeah, sure. pay for the Green Star Lake drug-runner to go to Winnipeg."

"Oh, come on, Jimmy. That's over. The council will support you."

Jimmy was relieved when Vincent came through the door. He gave Theresa a big hug and kiss, and then picked up Natasha and started singing to her, rocking her back and forth.

She spoke to Vincent. "So I asked Jimmy if he's going to Winnipeg to get his grade 11, but he won't answer me." Jimmy shook his head and ignored her.

"Yeah," Vincent said. "Does he ever tell anybody what he's thinking or what he's planning to do? The mystery man." They both enjoyed a laugh, but Jimmy got up, telling them he had to go to the store.

After Jimmy left, Theresa and Vincent sat at the table talking while Chance crawled up on his lap and Natasha fell asleep in her arms. Theresa asked her mother to take care of Natasha so she could go for a walk with Chance and Vincent. Vincent told her, "No, I don't know what he's going to do, but he seems different after his time in the bush and that wild snowmobile race."

"Yeah, you're right. He is different. I wonder how long it will last."

"He's not as wound up and mad. He's just not as wild and quick to get into a fight. Not so much that raging cowboy. I think Paul has something to do with it, too. I noticed it.

"I wasn't here, but you're right. He's a lot easier to talk to now. I don't have to be so careful about what I say."

"But who knows with him? He can change like the weather on a hot summer day."

"What are you going to do, Vincent?"

"I haven't told anybody this yet, but I'm going to Winnipeg next month to see what I can do with my music."

"That's great, Vincent."

"It's going to be tough. Really tough, Theresa. Lots of competition."

"But it's what you really want to do, isn't it?"

"True, but it's a little bit scary, Theresa. Gotta try to get on the right wave length."

"Hey, my life is pretty scary at times, Vincent."

"I know that. I thought about you when I was trying to decide whether to go or not."

"But you're so good at music."

"There's a ton of good singers out there."

"But you can write songs. Not just sing."

"That's why I want to try it. It be great if Jimmy was down there with us. If you're going back."

"I'm starting university in September. I've got to keep going as long as no huge problem comes up. I've got to keep going.

I'm afraid to stop. And not I might never get back on the plane again. Not become a nurse."

Vincent put his arm around Theresa as they walked back.

"I'm a little worried about Jimmy, Vincent."

"You're always all fired up about him."

It was true that she had always been afraid of the unknown with Jimmy. So many times she had seen him change from one person to someone else as if a switch had been flicked.

"I hope he doesn't start with the drugs again." Vincent didn't know how to answer that.

When Theresa landed in Winnipeg, she knew that the next time she got on the plane to Green Star Lake she'd have her grade 11.

CHAPTER 14

Bruce

Every couple of weeks, Arielle got an email from Bruce describing his travels. They were interesting, and she was glad for him but was uncomfortable when he wrote that he was hoping that they could spend some time together when he returned. Arielle was puzzled that Bruce would still care after all the months that had passed. Didn't he see that she was no longer interested? Bruce gave her the address where she could write to but Arielle never did. Her mind was on other things— school and her new friends and a new way of looking at the world around her. It all helped her get over her father's death and the break-up with Bruce. When she thought about next summer, Arielle decided that she was going to stay in Winnipeg and get a job, save some money and continue to meet new people. When she thought about Theresa, she felt an immediate sadness. Many times, she thought about phoning but never seemed to get around to it. She no longer heard from Theresa and understood why, when she recalled the way she had treated Theresa that last time they were together. Arielle knew that she had to sort out in her mind all that had happened in the past few months. Pushing Green Star Lake into the background seemed to be something she needed to do for the time being, so that she could get through this time in her life and move forward. Was Theresa going to be lost as a friend because of Arielle's need to be tough and independent?

Zach was spending less and less time at school, and he was very far behind, with little chance that he would pass his grade 10. When he did go to school, he often sat staring out the window, hoping that the spring would come and the weather would improve so that he could spend more days outside. His two teachers had him spend time with the resource teacher, who encouraged him and helped him with his inability to read beyond the most basic level. Zach understood what they were trying to do, but it was embarrassing that he could hardly read stories that most grade five students could handle easily. He saw his reading difficulty as an overwhelming, depressing challenge. He felt that the time had passed when he could keep up with his class. Being at the same level with other grade 10 students was not part of his reality anymore. That hope was gone, and Zach felt it was never coming back. So, why try? Why sit in school and pretend that he could succeed? It wasn't going to happen. On the days he turned up at school, he asked himself why he was sitting there. When he managed to spend a whole day at school, he was often agitated, and then relieved when he was finally able to leave after the last class. Sometimes, Zach wondered what had happened over the years. He remembered those early years at school, when he had enjoyed being in the classroom. He couldn't remember one thing that had happened to change it all. He simply felt a slowly growing distance from other students. It confused him, and he knew that there was little chance it would turn around.

On the days he attended school, Tracy would try to find him at the break or at the end of the day, but Zach didn't want to start looking forward to seeing her. Every time he saw Tracy, he felt a spark go through his chest, a spark he didn't want to feel, a spark he didn't want to trust. It scared him, yet he couldn't deny the flood of warmth that washed over his resistance when Tracy touched him on the arm, or squeezed his hand. Tracy knew that Zach struggled at school but never mentioned it or offered to help him. Something told Tracy not to bring it up, as if it could become an obstacle and push them apart. When they were together, Tracy often did most of the talking, not because she wanted to, but because the silences were long and uncomfortable for her. It's not that she thought Zach wasn't interested, but that he couldn't or wouldn't unlock what was going on in his head, even though she could tell from the look in his eyes that he wanted the connection. He never asked for anything or tried to come on to her. He always acted as if he didn't want to have anything to do with her being there beside him. In a strange way, Tracy found his attitude attractive and an interesting challenge. This time she had to be the one to make the relationship work, when she was so accustomed to boys chasing her. Tracy knew one thing for sure. She wanted Zach to respond the same way as other boys did. Zach, on the other hand, sensed somewhere in the back of his mind that Tracy was determined to get something he might not be willing to give up.

It was clear to Tracy that Zach was mostly interested in a life on the edge of criminality. She had heard him say on more than one occasion, "I'm not always going to be poor. I'm tired of being poor. I'll find a way to make money. Whatever I have to do. Anything."

He said this with such force and anger that Tracy found it unusual, because Zach so rarely spoke with any emotion or energy. She knew he had been involved in some break-ins and had been questioned by the band constables. She had a pretty good idea of what Zach meant by "whatever I have to do." The phrase was both a warning and a beckoning flame for her. Also, it gave her some knowledge that she could use to her advantage.

As the weather began to warm over Green Star Lake, Jimmy put away the Arctic Cat for the winter. Now he looked forward to being out in the boat with Chance. It would be a while before the ice was gone Jimmy saw himself heading up the lake, the wind blowing through his hair and the hum of his uncle's 30-horsepower pushing the boat into the morning sun.

Most days, he found himself wandering through the community, feeling the restlessness and urge to get something going. He was running out of money. He hated that because it made him feel helpless. He thought about how he could change that. He got a kick out of some of the ideas that Zach had suggested to him but never for a moment took him seriously. Zach was attracted to the easiest and fastest way to get cash. New ideas were slowly starting to creep into the back of Jimmy's mind. When they did, he thought about his talks with Paul, which struggled for equal time and space in his thinking. The two sides had been in conflict and balance for the past two years. On the days he sat on the dock in the warming sun, he thought about the excitement and adventure of last winter, when he was constantly trying to evade the police. He compared that experience to being in the race a few months ago. Adrenalin. He remembered that word from his science class. The high he got from facing danger, with the adrenalin running through his body. He missed that feeling and wanted to get it back. Jimmy knew it was something he needed in his life. Soon.

At the beginning of April, Bruce had been working for two weeks at a small hotel in southern France. He was finally able to put his high school French to use, and to use his English to assist the many tourists from Canada and the United States. The owner provided him with a room, meals and a small salary. Bruce told him he would stay until the end of August. Two weeks after starting work, he met a girl from Chicago who had a job taking care of three children for a family living 12 miles from the hotel. For the first time he began to think of someone other than Arielle.

He decided to send Arielle a letter.

Tracy was listening to Zach talk about his plans.

"I'd like to do something really big, you know, not just some break-in around here."

Tracy leaned over and kissed him on the neck and kept her arms tightly wound around his chest.

"Really big?" she asked.

"Yeah. Not some stupid, nothing theft around here. Anybody can do that." He didn't tell her that his goal was to impress Jimmy.

"So you'd have to leave here to do it, eh, Zach?" she encouraged him.

"Maybe Winnipeg."

"But how would you get there?"

"On the plane. I can't hitchhike outta here." They came up with a plan.

"Do you think I can do it?" he asked her.

"Why not? They always go into the building before the plane takes off. You could do it, especially if it's snowing."

"Yeah, and they leave the cargo door open until they're ready to leave."

"You can do it, Zach. I know you can."

When Tracy left, she gave Zach a long kiss. Zach wanted to hold on to her.

Zach walked home full of confidence and with the scent of Tracy's perfume still in his head.

Tracy headed to the back of the school to meet another boy. She took his hand as they walked down the road into the fading light. As they walked, she leaned toward him and kissed him while she listened to him complain about his brother. She squeezed his hand and smiled to herself.

CHAPTER 15

Zach's Trip

T hree days later, it was snowing heavily when the plane came into Green Star. Zach and Tracy stood behind the trees at the edge of bush lining the airstrip across from the terminal. Zach watched as everybody got off the plane and the cargo was unloaded. When the freight and baggage was loaded, the cargo door was left open in case any last-minute packages or passengers arrived. As often happened, the pilots walked into the Green Star Lake airport building with a clipboard to check everything off before leaving.

"Now. Now, Zach. Here's your chance."

"You'll wait for me, Tracy?" He searched her eyes.

"Zach. I'll be here. Where else? When you get back we can have some real fun."

That gave Zach a lift, and he sprinted across the 150 yards in the heavy snowfall toward the back of the plane. He could hardly make out the terminal. He felt his heart beating and his breath quickening.

Just another few yards, he said to himself. He ducked under the body of the plane and rushed to the other side of the plane. He watched the door of the terminal. He reached up with both hands and grabbed the bottom of the opening. After yanking himself up and into the cargo hold, he scrambled behind some boxes and pieces of baggage. A few minutes later, he heard the door slam and the two turbines wind up. He'd done it. In a couple of hours, he'd be in Winnipeg, trying to figure out a way to get away from the plane without getting caught. When he realized how cold it was going to be in the back of the plane, he opened a couple of suitcases and put on two sweaters.

Zach started to think about how he could return to Green Star Lake with some real cash.. He was not going back as part of the cargo. That wasn't going to happen.

Arielle finally phoned Theresa in April.

"Theresa, can you forgive me for the way I've been?"

"Oh, Arielle, you've had such a hard year. We've been friends since we were two years old. I didn't think we'd ever lose that."

"But I've been so cruel. Those things I said to you. You didn't deserve it."

"Are you going home this summer?"

"No. I'm going to find a job. for the summer.

"Too bad" Theresa told her.

"Can you come over this Saturday? I'm going to make supper for everybody at the house. You can meet my room-mates.

I promised them a northern meal."

"Yeah, sure, I'll be there. I'd like that, Arielle. Did you hear that Vincent is moving to Winnipeg?"

"When?"

"I"m not sure, but pretty soon."

"That'll be good to see him."

Arielle felt better when she got off the phone after hearing a voice that was so familiar and genuine.

When Jimmy arrived at Paul's cabin, the door was partially open. He stuck his head inside and called out to Paul. There was no answer. He was about to leave when he saw Paul sitting in a chair with his back to the door. When Jimmy went over to talk to Paul, he saw that his eyes were closed but his lips were moving as if he was whispering to Jimmy.

"Paul, are you okay?"

At first, Paul didn't answer. Jimmy waited, hoping Paul would know that he was in the room. At first he thought Paul was off in another world, but then began to realize that not only was he experiencing some difficulty breathing, but that he was looking very exhausted.

When Paul opened his eyes an hour later, Jimmy was sitting in a chair beside him.

"Were you sleeping?" Jimmy asked.

"Resting, Jimmy."

"You seem sick, Paul."

"Sick?"

"Yes. Very sick, or really tired, Paul."

"Yes. I am old, Jimmy. My time is passing now. My life has been good. Very good. It is time."

"What do you mean?" Jimmy asked, feeling the worry begin to build for this shaman, who had been so good to him, who had believed in him, who had been so patient in his teachings.

"You knew this time would come. Look around, Jimmy. All this is yours now—the cabin and everything in it. Some day you will know when you're ready to be here for the people. Move into this place, your place, when the time is right. You have the gift."

"No, Paul. I'll take you to the nursing station."

"No, Jimmy. I know what's best for me right now. Read for me from your notes when you were in the bush. Tell me about what you experienced."

Jimmy read from his notes and then talked for more than two hours, describing his experiences and travels through other dimensions. Paul smiled and nodded several times. After some time had passed, Jimmy noticed that Paul had become very quiet and motionless. Jimmy called his name but got no response. He knew Paul had quietly passed on to another world. Jimmy felt the sadness begin to overcome him, and he started to think about what he would expect of himself now.

———•◆•———